THE WHITE OWL OF THICKLEWOOD HALL

Trussel and Gout: Paranormal Investigations No. 3

M.A.Knights

White Harp Publishing

Copyright © 2022 M.A.Knights

All rights reserved

The characters and events portrayed in this book are fictitious. Any similarity to real persons, living or dead, is coincidental and not intended by the author.

No part of this book may be reproduced, or stored in a retrieval system, or transmitted in any form or by any means, electronic, mechanical, photocopying, recording, or otherwise, without express written permission of the publisher.

ISBN-13: 9798838028310
ISBN-10: 1477123456

Cover design by M.A.Knights. Images from Shutterstock.com
Library of Congress Control Number: 2018675309
Printed in the United States of America

*To my parents
who nurtured my love of stories.*

CONTENTS

Title Page
Copyright
Dedication
Part One   1
Part Two   18
Part Three   30
Part Four   60
Part Five   72
Part Six   95
Part Seven   120
Free Book   129
More books by M.A.Knights   131
Acknowledgement   133
About The Author   135

PART ONE

I had seen death before. Most have, in one form or another. An aged or a young relative, perhaps. An unfortunate accident. It weaves into the fabric of our lives and we, being the remarkable species that we are, find ways to normalise it. The searing pain of loss is dulled by the passing of time. We continue. Yes, I thought I understood death. But the events at Thicklewood Hall would show me a side of death I had never experienced before. They would also show me a side to Mr Gout that would forever change my perception of the man I called my master.

We had been called to Thicklewood by a mysterious letter, arriving on the doormat of Oystercatcher Cottage just the week before. It had been short on details, but claimed that a great calamity had befallen the estate and it urgently needed Mr Gout's assistance. Despite Mrs Winchester's misgivings – and indeed my own – Mr Gout had insisted on going to the Hall as requested.

'I cannot, in all good conscience, ignore a call for aid,' he explained, and so we'd set off. But as the lonely miles went by, I realised that there was something about the letter that had unsettled my master. He did not voice his concerns to me, but I could tell. The spring was missing from his usually sprightly step, and he passed long periods in brooding silence.

Now, as the third day of our journey was drawing to a close, our wagon rumbled along the darkening road and a thickening canopy of branches arched over our heads. I sat next to Mr Gout, who held the reins, and our horse, a weary-looking thing we'd picked up in the nearest village, nosed his way forward towards our destination. January still clinched the world in its icy grasp, although its days were numbered. I did my best not to shiver, even though our breaths came in little puffs and my nose felt like it might soon fall off.

An owl called from somewhere in the branches above. It was a lonely sound, and I gave in to the shiver at last.

'Are we close yet, do you think?' I ventured.

Mr Gout, who seemed in little better spirits, nodded forcefully and, without letting go of the reigns, rubbed his large hands together to warm them. 'It can't be far now, my dear,' he said. 'Thicklewood Hall must be coming up soon. This road cannot go on forever!'

I was not so convinced. The road had certainly seemed to be doing its best to go on forever all afternoon, and I saw no real reason why it should stop now.

It had been a long and tiring journey north through unfamiliar country for one so little travelled as my younger self. But we were finally within reaching distance of the estate and I looked forward to a proper bed that night. The inns we stayed at had been chosen by my master because of their homely nature. 'Homely', I soon learnt, meant cheap. Last night's metal bed frame had left what seemed an irreversible impression on my back. It must have been far worse for my master. I had recently discovered he was suffering from the effects of a curse that rendered him incapable of sleeping under any permanent roof. This meant he had spent the last few nights sleeping in whatever shed, outhouse, or temporary building he could find at each of our stops. It had also seemed to affect aspects of his memory – most importantly, perhaps, the location of his own home. It was all very peculiar, and something I intended to find out more about during our trip to Thicklewood Hall. However, given Mr Gout's sombre mood, the opportunity had not yet presented itself. I was beginning to doubt it ever would.

As I thought this, the aforementioned Hall finally came into view. We had been following a long, high stone wall on our right for some time now and without warning it suddenly fell away, to be replaced by a pair of even taller iron gates. Through them, we caught our first glimpse of the Hall. It was of Georgian design: a neat, if somewhat grandiose, box of a building with large pillars to the front and a sweeping set of steps that led down to a gravel driveway. It was still some way off, shuttered behind its walls and gates like some exotic animal in a zoo, cowering in the far corner of its cage. Yes, cowering. For even at that first glance, there was something about the place that seemed...off. It is wrong perhaps to say that a building can look scared, but if ever one did, it was Thicklewood.

Mr Gout let the cart trundle past the gates without slowing, and soon the Hall became lost to sight once more. For the letter had been very clear in one thing; we were to report to the gamekeeper's cottage and not to approach the main house directly. This was not particularly unusual. We were, after all, the servants in this scenario, but something about the request sat unwell with me. Normally servants would be told to report to the back entrance, not to the gamekeeper's cottage. It was also a slight mystery exactly who had written the letter summoning us. They had signed simply it 'Mr Harding'. Who Mr Harding was we had not yet discovered, but we were about to.

We continued on our way, the cart rattling along what was little more than a dirt track that still ran besides the forbidding estate wall. Above us the tree canopy grew thicker, and the twisted arms of ancient oaks, turned almost green with moss in the damp air, blocked out most of what little light remained. Dusk approached ahead of schedule.

We turned a corner, still following the wall, and eventually caught sight of the cottage we had been directed to. It was a small building, attached to the estate wall itself and made of the same sandy-grey stone. It had a somewhat dishevelled appearance, an effect created by the dozens of wooden carvings that littered the grass in front of the cottage, seemingly abandoned. They ranged from some the size of a large dog to some as small as mice. Animals were very much the unifying theme. There were pigs, birds, foxes, hedgehogs, snakes, the remains of what must have been some sort of bear, and everything in between. Some were new, the wood bright and looking freshly cut. But many others were obviously much older, covered in moss and lichen, or almost completely rotted away. They might have been quite jolly, in the right circumstances. As it was, they lent the cottage a somewhat…well. One hesitates to use the word 'creepy' to describe anybody's home…but if the shoe fits. I couldn't help but wonder why they had been left there.

The cottage roof was thatched, and my heart sank as we drew closer. It was not large enough to contain more than a single bedroom. Perhaps the night of relative comfort I hoped for was not to be. As Mr Gout pulled on the reins, and our less than sprightly horse gratefully stumbled to a halt outside the building, its wooden door opened and a man strode out to meet us.

The first thing I noticed about him was the thick, black-grey beard that stood out from his thin face like the bristles of a broom. His brow was heavy, and he frowned at us as he approached, looking up to where we sat on the driver's bench with beady, deep-set eyes.

'Mr Gout?' he said, his voice harsh, croaking as though it had not been used for a year.

If my master took offence at the man's lack of manners, he did not show it. 'Indeed!' he responded with his usual gaiety. 'Do I have the honour of addressing Mr Harding?'

The man nodded. 'Aye, that's me. Gamekeeper of Thicklewood Estate. You're late.'

Mr Gout's eyebrows rose a fraction of an inch. 'It has been a long journey,' was all he said and began the slow process of removing his bulk from the wagon and depositing it onto the ground. I jumped down, ran around the wagon, and offered him my arm as he descended.

'Bless you, my dear girl,' he said, then turned to Mr Harding. 'So, here we are, here we are…. I must say, your letter was a little cryptic to the exact, err…nature of why you have summoned us.'

Mr Handing ran a shaking hand through his beard, glancing nervously up into the trees as he did so. ''Tis a dark, dark affair, Mr Gout. Very dark indeed.'

'Oh yes?' said Mr Gout pleasantly, massaging his prodigious behind and arching his back to unlock the effects of the long drive. 'Perhaps we could discuss it over a nice cup of tea?'

Mr Harding's face darkened further. 'I'm not

paying you to sit around and drink tea!'

Mr Gout blinked at him. 'As of yet, my good man, you are not paying me to do anything. I know nothing about you or this case and have made no decision as to whether I shall decide to act in the matter. What I have decided, however, is that if there is no tea to be had for weary travellers at the end of a long day *here*, then I shall climb back aboard this wagon right now and persuade this frankly exhausted nag to pull it back to the nearest hospitable house I can find. The question then shall be if I decide to return – and I have to tell you, Mr Harding, I fear it would be doubtful.'

He said all this with a perfectly amiable smile on his circular face, but I had known the man for some three months or so now, and was beginning to sense the almost invisible changes in his demeanour that foretold his coming anger. A certain set of the shoulders. A tiny widening of the smile. Mr Harding was treading on very thin ice.

Luckily, the gamekeeper seemed to sense this and relented. 'Alright, alright. No offence meant, mister. I'll get the kettle on in a minute, alright?'

'Splendid!' Mr Gout beamed with genuine pleasure.

'But this is a serious business, sir, you must understand that,' the gamekeeper continued, glancing again into the hanging branches above our heads, before peering into my master's face earnestly. 'I fear for the safety of those on the estate.'

Mr Gout's face became serious. 'I see. You must

tell me all about it. But after the tea.'

Mr Harding didn't seem to catch the last part, or if he did, chose to ignore it, his gaze once more drifting to the treetops. It lingered there when he spoke next, in a hushed voice. 'There is a terrible curse upon these woods, Mr Gout. A terrible, terrible curse. You've come just in time. For you see, we are besieged, sir.'

'Is that so?' Mr Gout looked unimpressed, his own gaze drifting to the tiny cottage and no doubt imagining what comfort and refreshment it might contain.

As each man seemed ill disposed to give his full attention to the other, I decided I should unload our bags from the wagon. There were few, in truth, and most belonged to Mr Gout, who I was not entirely surprised to learn travelled nowhere without at least three suitcases to sustain him.

The gamekeeper seemed unaware of my master's less than enthusiastic attitude towards his story and continued, his eyes constantly searching the darkening branches of the many oaks that lined the road and surrounded the cottage. 'It comes at night,' he said. 'A terror from hell.'

'I don't suppose it brings biscuits?' Mr Gout muttered, his good grace finally slipping.

Mr Hasting whirled round on him with a fierceness that I fancy surprised Mr Gout and made me drop the suitcase I'd been handling.

'This is no joking matter!' he hissed, spittle flying from his mouth. 'We're dealing with pure evil here. A spirit from the darkest depths of this accursed woodland! If it isn't stopped, there's no telling the damage it could do!'

Mr Gout did indeed look startled by the proclamation, but he had taken a distinct dislike to the gamekeeper by this point, and he simply arched an eyebrow. 'An evil spirit?' he said, clearly unconvinced. 'And what shape, pray tell, does the ferocious force take?'

An owl hooted in the trees above and Mr Harding's head whipped up to face the canopy so fast it surprised me he didn't strain his neck. 'It's here,' he said through tightly clenched teeth. 'It's come! You can see for yourself!'

I looked at him, perplexed, then I realised what he meant. 'The owl?' I said. 'You're being terrorised by an owl?'

The bird called again, a long, haunting sound that cut through the growing dusk of the woodland. I turned to my master, expecting to see the same look of scoffing disbelief on his face that my own no doubt held, but instead found him peering into the branches with a new intensity. The owl called a third time, and this time there was an edge to the noise. Some discordant sound that made me, too, peer into the skeletal limbs of the oaks above our heads.

'Be aware, Clementine, my dear,' said Mr Gout, all annoyance gone from his voice, which now held an urgent tone of warning.

I caught a movement to my right and turned to see the silent, ghostly figure of a bird gliding through the limbs of a tree not one hundred paces away. It was indeed an owl. A large one at that, and so pure a white that it almost dazzled my eyes in the gathering gloom. It disappeared back into the darkness of the wood. For a moment, there was silence, before an ear-splitting shriek rent the air, now only just discernible as an owl. Our horse stamped the ground and whinnied nervously.

'What is this?' Mr Gout demanded, turning angrily on our host.

'It is the spirit!' the man gushed, his little eyes popping from his head. 'The devil of Thicklewood! I told you! I told you it would come!'

'A devil?' Mr Gout burst out, his voice echoing in the stillness that seemed to fall in the owl's wake. 'That's not–'

But he was cut short by another ear-rending shriek that cut to the very core of my body and cooled my blood. Then the brilliant white shape of the owl erupted from the shadows once more, at speed this time, and heading right for us.

'Run!' Mr Harding yelled. 'Run, you fools!'

I felt rooted to the spot. I could now see clearly the face of the oncoming bird. It was completely white. Even the rounds of its eyes were of a milky hue, and as it drew near, it unsheathed a set of long, pure white talons that it thrust in our direction as its flight became a dive. I tripped over my own feet in my hurry to get away. Mr Gout gave a squawk of alarm and did an awkward pirouette in mid-air as the thing streaked down towards him and he attempted to jump out of the way. He only just managed it, the bird's fierce talons raking the very top of his head as it passed. The bird pulled up sharply before it hit the ground and swooped back up into the air with a shriek.

'Into the house!' the gamekeeper cried, helping Mr Gout to his feet and all but shoving him in the cottage's direction. I fled too, looking back over my shoulder to see that the owl had turned and was readying for another dive. My feet pounded up the gravel path to the little wooden front door that was still hanging partly open, and I threw myself through, holding it open for the two men who were hot on my heels. When we were all three safely inside, I slammed the door closed with considerable relief and rushed to the nearest window, peering out into the twilight to get a glimpse of our attacker.

'I told yer!' Mr Harding was screaming, jigging up and down excitedly. 'Didn't I tell yer? A beast the thing is, a demon! Maybe you'll believe me now, eh? Maybe you'll take me seriously now?'

Mr Gout mumbled something incoherent, and I turned from the window just long enough to see him mopping at his head with a handkerchief that was coming away stained with blood.

Mr Harding was warming to his theme, spittle flying from his mouth once again as he jumped and gesticulated wildly. 'You see what we are faced with, Mr Gout? D'yer see now why not a soul dares to go abroad across the entire estate once darkness comes? Well, man? What have you got to say for yourself?'

Mr Gout seemed more annoyed than anything else, and he fixed the erratic gamekeeper with a baleful gaze as he patted gently at his scalp. 'What I have to say, Mr Harding, is that clearly there is something going on here which you have not been kind enough to completely explain. I have been in this line of business for some considerable time, Mr Harding, and may I tell you that never before have I had my delicate pate raked by the enraged talons of an owl, demon or no. I was once defecated on by a pigeon, but that is par for the course in the countryside, and certainly not limited to members of my profession.'

Mr Harding seemed hardly to be listening, however, having worked himself up into a temper.

'Demon owl, demon owl!' he kept repeating, emphasising the words with wild sweeps of his sinewy arms.

I returned my attention to the dark woods outside, and I fancied I could make out the pale glow of the ferocious bird in question, sitting high in the branches of an oak that stood sixty yards or so from the cottage. Night had fallen almost completely now, and I shuddered at the ghostly sight of it. It didn't seem to move, but I felt like it was watching me, waiting. Our horse, still tethered to the wagon, was pacing an uncertain circle. Then another movement caught my eye.

A young blond woman, not much older than myself, was walking towards the cottage. She looked like a maid, most likely coming down from the main house, and was carrying a basket covered with a cloth. She walked in the unhurried way of one who has escaped from their workplace for a few precious moments and intends to make the most of it. Of the owl, she seemed entirely unaware.

'There's somebody out there,' I said.

The two men rushed to the window, and Mr Harding cursed harshly in his croaky voice. 'The foolish girl! I told her not to be out after dark. We must do something at once!' Without waiting for an answer, he grasped a walking stick from where it leaned on the wall, flung himself towards the door and had opened it and sprung through before either Mr Gout or myself could object. He ran out of the cottage, waving his arms above his head and making such a din it was a wonder the very trees did not complain about the noise.

'Away! Away with you, silly girl! The winged beast is abroad and ye are in grave peril! Away!'

The owl launched itself from its perch and plummeted towards them. Our horse squealed and reared up on its hind legs. The girl started and dropped her basket.

'Come, Clementine!' Mr Gout cried, and I followed him out of the door, anxious to do something, but unsure of exactly what.

Mr Harding reached the woman and grabbed her roughly by the shoulders. 'Do ye want to die, foolish girl?' he screamed. Her face was an astonished 'o' of surprise, but before she could speak he had released her and spun round to face the bird that had now closed the distance between them and was diving once more, talons extended. The gamekeeper gave a cry of rage and brandished the stick at the bird, missing, but causing the creature to alter its course and veer off to one side. Unfortunately, the maid had stumbled away from Mr Harding in shock and the bird collided with her in a flurry of shrieks, feathers and a flash of talons. The owl wheeled away and then shot up into the trees, out of sight. The girl fell to the ground, clutching her face.

Mr Gout and I arrived as Mr Harding dropped the stick and bent to help the girl, who was now wailing something fierce.

Mr Gout reached the man just in time to place a beefy hand on his shoulder. 'Allow me,' he said, holding the gamekeeper back and taking his place by the stricken woman's side as she sobbed freely. Her hands still covered her face, so it was hard to see what damage the owl might have done, but a trickle of cherry-red blood dripped between her fingers.

I scanned the tree canopy nervously, searching for the white glow of the owl, but I saw no sign. Perhaps it had retreated for now. It was fully dark by this point and increasingly difficult to make out the shapes of the trees. I felt exposed out in the open.

Mr Gout knelt down beside the sobbing maid and laid a soothing hand gently upon her shoulder. 'There, there,' he said. 'The creature has gone.'

The woman jumped slightly at his touch, removing her hands from her face just enough to get a look at him. 'Who…who are you?'

'This here is Mr Gout, girl! He's the paranormal investigator what I called for. He'll see to that damned owl! He'll send it back to the pits of hell from which it came! He'll–'

'That's quite enough of that,' Mr Gout cut in, interrupting the man's diatribe before he could scare the poor woman any further. 'Now, my dear, let me have a look at your face. Let us see what can be done.' He beamed down at the maid, his round face shining at her in that irresistible way I was beginning to find familiar, and ever so gently prised her trembling hands away from her face. She let it happen, staring up at his friendly features with the same wonder, the same slightly numb expression I had seen so many people give my master.

The cuts to her face were not as bad as I had feared. They ran in three parallel lines down the very centre of her face, the middle cut ending at the very tip of her nose, the other two continuing down onto her white cheeks. They were clean but deep and might well scar.

'Ooh, tut, tut. Not to worry, my dear. Nothing a little time and attention won't fix. Let us get you into the cottage, hmm? A little something to steady the nerves, perhaps?' Mr Gout helped the woman to her feet.

'What was that thing?' she said.

'It was that devil owl, Sally! You should have

known better than to be wandering about at this time. I *told* you all to be careful!'

Sally looked confused and opened her mouth to speak, but Mr Harding waved away her objections before she could utter them.

'No time for that now, girl. We need to get you back to the main house. We can take your wagon,' he said, turning to Mr Gout, who looked less than happy at the suggestion.

'The cottage is much closer,' he reasoned. 'And I think–'

'I ain't paying you to drink tea and I ain't paying you to play nursemaid neither,' Mr Harding snapped, grabbing Sally by the arm and pulling her none too gently towards our wagon. Our horse eyed him suspiciously and stamped its feet.

Mr Gout opened his mouth to object, but Sally caught his eye, shaking her head. 'It... it's alright, mister,' she said through the sobs that still racked her body. 'I'd best be getting back or they'll be wondering where I've got to.' Her face dropped even further as a thought hit her. She scanned the ground until her eyes alighted upon the basket she'd been carrying, which was now lying a way off. The remains of a meal had spilled out across the grass. 'Oh no! Your dinner, Mr Harding, it's ruined!'

'Never mind that, stupid girl!' the gamekeeper said. 'Let's go.' He hoisted the maid up onto the seating platform and scurried up behind her, grabbing the reins as he went. Once seated, he looked down at Mr Gout and said, 'I'll have your horse stabled up at the house. You two had better take shelter in my cottage for now.'

'Surely we should come with you and–' Mr Gout replied, but it was too late. The man had already whipped the reins and got the startled horse to move off at a canter down the road towards the house, leaving the two of us alone in the dark.

Mr Gout watched the wagon disappear, his hands on his hips. 'Well, my dear,' he said. 'A fine pickle we find ourselves in. I suppose we had better return to the cottage as ordered. Before any more creatures of the forest attack us.'

PART TWO

Thirty minutes later, we were safely concealed within the gamekeeper's cottage once more. Not currently being under attack, I had a chance to inspect the place for the first time. It was not large. There was one room that served as an entrance hall, living room, kitchen and mudroom all in one. Behind a wooden door lay the only other room, presumably where Mr Harding slept. It was what my father would politely call a typical single man's abode. My mother would have called it a bloody disgrace. Mr Harding clearly lived alone. Dirty clothes littered the floor, dirtier dishes filled the small sink, and what I can only describe as an absolutely filthy rag-work rug covered the small rectangle of floor that lay between the lone wingback chair and the fireplace. I had stoked the fire and set a kettle above the flames. A rudimentary search of Mr Harding's cupboards had resulted in little to offer us for dinner, but I did find a tin of biscuits.

Mr Gout was making his way through them at a steady pace, but with little sign of his usual enjoyment. His mouth moved mechanically as he stared into the flames of the fire, his hand dipping back into the tin without a glance in its direction when each biscuit ran out. He had said little in the last half hour and I was worrying. He seemed… unsettled.

I confess, I was more than a little shaken. I had always rather liked owls, but was now making some hasty readjustments of my opinion. But it was unusual for my master to be so affected. I had seen him tackle a zombie without hesitation, but there was something bothering him now. The owl had shaken him too, and that worried me all the more.

When the kettle whistled, I took it down and made tea. The gamekeeper's cups were filthy, but I got the worst off the cleanest-looking pair and served one to Mr Gout, who barely glanced up to acknowledge it. Growing concerned, I cleared my throat awkwardly. 'Is everything alright, sir?'

'Hmm,' he said, adjusting his head a little in my direction, but not quite removing his gaze from the fire. I repeated the question, walking between him and the fireplace, breaking the almost hypnotic hold it seemed to have over him. He sat back with a start and his glazed eyes eventually focused on my face.

'I'm so very sorry, my dear. What were you saying?' He gave me a half smile.

'I was simply asking if you were alright,' I said

for the third time, truly worried now.

'Oh, yes, yes. Fine…fine.' He fell silent again, his eyes sliding from my face once more. I was about to rebuke him when he suddenly brought one of his enormous fists down on the arm of his chair with a crack. 'There is something badly wrong on this estate,' he said. 'And I intend to find out what it is!' He lifted his eyes to mine again, and I saw an anger burning there with a fierceness I had never seen in the man before.

Startled, I said, 'Do you think that Mr Hastings is right? Is the owl some kind of demonic force?'

'Pha!' he spat, picking up his tea and sloshing a good portion on the rug in his anger. 'You will find, my dear, that people always turn to tales of monsters and demons when they are trying to cover up much more earthly wrongdoings. That owl is no demon or devil of the forest.'

'Oh, well, that's a relief,' I said.

'Oh no,' Mr Gout continued. 'It's much more sinister than that!'

My heart fell.

'It's a ghost!' Mr Gout said forcefully, attempting to take a sip of his tea and pouring half of it in his lap.

I was confused. 'A ghost? Do you mean the ghost of an owl? But I've never known an owl to act like that and besides, what about Custard?'

Custard, in case you haven't read my earlier transcription of my adventures with Mr Gout, is the ghost of his pet rabbit. He is mischievous, certainly, and has been known to torment Mrs Winchester, Mr Gout's elderly housekeeper, occasionally, but he has certainly never attacked anyone. And the owl…well, it had emanated a malevolence I had never felt from Custard.

'Oh no, no, you quite misunderstand,' Mr Gout said, attempting to dab at the wet patch on his legs with a handkerchief. 'This is not the ghost of any animal; this is the ghost of a human. And one who died in tragic circumstances at that.'

'A human? But then why…'

'Does it look like an owl? That is an excellent question, and one we must endeavour to answer if we are to solve this mystery, my dear. No, this isn't any normal ghost…'

He paused for a moment, looking pensive. It gave me time to reflect on the fact that anyone might consider *any* type of ghost normal.

Mr Gout continued. 'What I fear we are dealing with here is a powerful vengeful spirit. A revenant. Quite another cup of tea all together. I never thought I'd see one again.'

He paused once more, his eyes drawn back to the fire.

'So you've come across a ghost…a revenant like this before?' I asked, hoping to stop his mind from slipping away from me again.

He didn't turn from the fire, staring deep, deep into the orange flame. It was some time before he replied, so long in fact that I had almost given up hope he would. 'Oh yes,' he said. 'Once…only once, a very long time ago.'

He did not elaborate.

Mr Harding eventually returned some time later. I had elicited little in the way of conversation from my master after the talk of vengeful spirits, so it was with almost thankful optimism that I saw the grouchy gamekeeper coming up the garden path. He opened the door and came inside, stamping his feet on the mat and rubbing his hands together.

'Bloody cold out there.'

'Is the maid alright? Sally, wasn't it?' I asked.

Mr Harding looked at me as if he had completely forgotten I existed. 'Hmm? Oh, yes, yes. I got her settled up at the house. Your horse too. Not the most sprightly of beasts, is it?' This last he addressed to Mr Gout, who responded by giving him a baleful glare and asking a question of his own.

'Who died?'

Mr Harding looked taken aback. 'I'm sorry?'

'I asked you who died?' Mr Gout repeated. I was really worrying about him now. The anger that showed on his face seemed alien there, like an emotion from some other person, superimposed on the face of my affable master.

'I know somebody died,' he continued. 'And I know it was not a pleasant death. So who was it?'

Mr Harding bristled. 'I told yer, no one! What are yer on about?'

'Well, that is strange, Mr Harding, very strange indeed. Queer, one might even say. Because, you see, that owl is a revenant, and a revenant is only created when someone dies. Murdered, most often, and in considerable emotional distress. It is not every day that a revenant is created. They are rare, Mr Harding. Very rare. So I will ask you one last time, who died?'

The gamekeeper eyed him nastily. 'If I said no one died, then no one died! I don't know what yer on about revenants for. I told yer what it is. It's a demon! Now are yer gonna do something about it, or yer gonna keep bothering me with this nonsense?'

Mr Gout had by this time got to his feet, and the two men faced each other down. Then, to my utter surprise, Mr Gout's face split into a beaming smile. 'Quite right, Mr Harding, quite right. My mistake entirely. Of course, if no one has died, then it stands to reason we must be dealing with a demon, just as you say.'

Mr Harding looked as taken aback as I was at the sudden change in my master's demeanour, but he nodded curtly. 'That's right,' he said.

'Well, perhaps you will be so good as to furnish me with all the details?' Mr Gout said. 'If I am properly to banish the demon, then I must have all the facts correct.'

'Alright,' said the gamekeeper, taking off his coat and hanging it on a peg by the door. 'What do yer need to know?'

'Come, come, sit by the fire and we can discuss it.' Mr Gout clapped the man jovially on the shoulder.

Mr Harding took the seat by the fire. He

observed the used kettle and cups and seemed about to say something, but then obviously thought better of it. Mr Gout stood, warming his backside by the flames.

Mr Harding looked my way. 'Should she be here for this?' he asked. 'Ain't no decent subject for a woman to be involved in.'

'You'll find Miss Clementine has a stomach stronger than most, be they male or female,' Mr Gout replied, offering me a smile, before returning his full attention to the man sitting in front of him. 'Let us start, Mr Harding, with the time and date of the owl's first appearance.'

Mr Harding looked thoughtful. 'Let's see now…must have been near four weeks back now, when I first caught sight of the loathsome beast. Just coming back from the woods, I was, where I'd been out cutting firewood. It caught my eyes at first because, well, you've seen it – unnaturally pale, it is. It perched there in that tree opposite the door to the cottage. I remember thinking it was odd because owls are usually secretive birds, not taken to sitting out in the open like that. Anyway, when I walked past I felt like I could feel it watching me… thought I was just being a damn fool at the time. I went inside and got on with things, only the next time I looked out the window, when I went to draw the curtains, it was still there. Sitting exactly where I'd seen it before, just staring at the house. Gave me chills, I don't mind telling you. Well, I went to bed and when I got up the next morning, it was gone. I forgot all about it after that, to tell the truth, until that evening when I got back to the cottage and there it was again. This time, I was sure it was watching me. I tried to scare it away, 'cos I didn't like the look of it, but no matter how much I shouted or waved my arms, it didn't move a muscle. Just stared with those horrible white eyes. Now you tell me if that ain't odd behaviour for an owl, Mr Gout.'

'Indeed,' Mr Gout said, motioning for him to continue.

'Well, this went on for about a week. Every night I got home and every night there it was. Till one night I was walking past it, doing my best to ignore the wretched thing as had become my custom, and it hooted at me.' The gamekeeper tugged at his beard distractedly and glared first at my master and then at me, as if daring us to laugh. 'Now, I ain't no coward, but there's something unnatural about the noises that thing makes. It ain't...well, it don't sound like no ordinary owl is what I'm saying.'

'Did it do anything else?' Mr Gout asked.

The gamekeeper shook his head. 'Not that night. Din't move, din't make another peep. But I tell you I could feel it watching me, even through the curtains. Even when I went to bed, I'd swear I could feel its eyes on me. After that, things got a little worse each night. It would make more and more noise, getting itself all worked up. Sounds like you ain't never heard. Then, about a week ago, just before I wrote to you, it attacked for the first time.

After that I went to the master and I told him it wasn't safe for people to be out in the estate at night. I don't know where it came from, Mr Gout, and I don't care to know. It's evil. I can feel it in my bones. Yer saw what it did to poor Sally. Yer got to get rid of it! Banish it back to whatever pit it slunk out of!'

Mr Harding looked at us expectantly, like he wanted us to whip out some sort of demon-vanishing wand right there and then.

Mr Gout stroked his round chin thoughtfully. 'Very interesting. Very interesting indeed. And you have no idea where it might have come from? No idea where it goes during the day? Where it might be right now? You got to the house and back unmolested, I notice.'

Mr Harding scowled. 'I just told yer, din't I? I ain't got no idea where it goes. Probably scared it off before. But it'll be back, you mark my words! So are yer going to help or not?'

Mr Gout sat back in his chair. 'Oh, certainly we will, Mr Harding, have no fear of that.'

'Good,' said the gamekeeper, getting to his feet. 'That's that, then. I'll be off to bed. You'd best make yourselves comfortable here till it comes back.'

'Wait, you expect us to deal with the thing tonight?' I blurted out in surprise. It had been a long few days, and I was already aching for sleep.

'Certainly I do!' Mr Harding said. 'That's why yer here!'

Mr Gout calmly placed his fingers together into a steeple over his belly. 'That, I'm afraid to say, will be out of the question.'

'Whaddya mean?'

'Work of this nature is delicate, Mr Harding. We cannot simply go out there and hit the thing with a broom. We shall need to observe. To investigate.'

The gamekeeper looked deeply unhappy about this, but he waved Mr Gout's words away with an irritable hand. 'Well, whatever, just get the job done. I'm off.'

'Off?' Mr Gout looked surprised.

'Well, I ain't sleeping here with you two. I'll go back to the house and find somewhere.'

'You mean for me and Miss Trussel to sleep…where exactly? There is but the one bedroom in your cottage, Mr Harding, and it would be far from proper–'

'This ain't some hotel, Mr Gout! Yer here to do a job. Get it done and be on your way!'

With that, the man stormed out, slamming the door behind him in Mr Gout's astonished face. I watched him stalk up the dark pathway, away from the cottage.

'Well, in all my years…' Mr Gout began, but seemed unable to finish the sentence.

'There is something very fishy about all this, sir,' I said, as the gamekeeper's form disappeared into the gloom.

'Fishy?' said Mr Gout. 'I should say there are many things about this that are fishy! In fact, the whole thing stinks so much it should not surprise me to wake up and find I had fainted in a fishmongers! But to what exactly were you referring, my dear?'

'Well, he claims to fear the owl and what it might do, but first he risks taking the maid, Sally, all the way to the main house, then coming back alone on foot. He is here barely twenty minutes and then decides he's off to the house again. For someone who claims to be afraid of something jumping out at him in the dark, he doesn't seem to mind walking around alone out there.'

My master nodded. 'You are quite right. His behaviour, apart from being boorish in the extreme, is incredibly suspicious. He is lying to us, I fear, and about a good many things, I should wager. Someone *was* killed here. I know it. There is no other logical explanation. Tomorrow morning, my dear Clementine, we shall have a great deal of investigating to do.'

'And in the meantime?' I ventured. Whilst I had no doubt that Mr Gout was a perfect gentleman, I had not forgotten about his predicament. He could not sleep under the gamekeeper's roof.

'You take the bedroom,' Mr Gout said, easing his frame back into the chair now vacated by Mr Harding. 'I shall make the best of it here by the fire.'

'But you must be exhausted, sir,' I began to protest, but he waved me away.

'I shall be quite alright. Besides…I have a good deal of thinking to do.'

His eyes returned to the fire and he would say no more.

PART THREE

The next morning came cold and grey. I had not slept well, despite taking the gamekeeper's bedroom. It was not...well, to be perfectly honest, I care little to recall the state of the room. Thoughts of my master kept me awake. There was still much I did not know about Mr Gout. I had grown used to the mystery that he wore like a cloak, but the events of the night before had reawakened many questions. I came into the main room to find him standing, still fully dressed in last night's clothes and staring out of the window. He turned as I entered and smiled.

'A very good morning to you, Clementine, my dear. I shall not ask if you slept well, for I fear that would be too much to wish for. However, I hope this morning finds you a little refreshed?'

His mood seemed to have lifted with new day and it was the old, cheerful Mr Gout who helped me search the cupboards once again for some kind of breakfast. His mood did lower when our searching revealed nothing but the ends of a very stale loaf of bread, but he bore the discovery with surprising grace and suggested we get started on our day.

Of Mr Harding, there was no sign.

We washed as best we could and headed out into the damp morning. My eyes were immediately drawn to the canopy of oaks, but apart from a fat little pigeon that cooed at us as we passed there was no sign of any bird life.

'The owl did not return last night,' Mr Gout informed me. 'Perhaps it is elsewhere in the forest, or perhaps it was frightened off by last night's events. I doubt that, however. Revenants do not frighten easily.'

'Do you mean to say you kept a lookout all night?' I asked with some surprise.

Mr Gout nodded. 'It does not pay to let one's guard down in these situations.'

'But you should have woken me!' I protested. 'I could have taken a turn.'

'I would not dream of having done so,' Mr Gout said. 'I fear our first proper investigation together will have done little to endear you to the life of a paranormal investigator so far, and should not like to have added sleep deprivation to the list.'

I decided not to tell him I had lain awake most of the night anyway and the subject was dropped. But, I thought, as we walked the gravelly path, following the estate wall back toward the main gates, it was further proof of just how worried my master was about the owl.

We reached the gates and found them firmly closed.

'Well, this is hardly the friendliest country house I've visited, I must say,' said Mr Gout, his mouth making a little moue of displeasure. 'Hullo?' he called, cupping his chubby hands around his mouth and calling through the wrought iron bars. There was no response.

Mr Gout tutted. 'It's almost as if the entire place were locked up.'

'What should we do?' I asked.

'Well, dear Clementine, I do hate to be a bad influence on the youth, but I'm afraid we may have to "Hop the fence" so to speak.'

I looked at the wall, which must have been a good seven feet tall, unconvinced.

Mr Gout must have read the thoughts on my face.

'Oh, don't be so pessimistic, my dear! It shall take but a jiffy.'

It took several jiffies. In fact, it took a great deal of effort, two skinned elbows, a bashed knee and an unfortunate ripping to the seat of Mr Gout's tweed trousers. But after the span of several minutes, we stood on the other side of the unfriendly gates, intact, if in somewhat more depressed spirits than when we had started the venture.

Mr Gout's mood, in particular, had taken a turn for the worse again. He twisted round himself and attempted to eye the damage to his trousers, muttering, not quite under his breath, 'And all before breakfast! If this is how a country estate treats its guests, I fear this entire country is going to the dogs!' He abandoned his pursuit and sighed heavily. 'What I wouldn't give for a cup of tea and a couple of kippers.'

'Perhaps we can find some breakfast up in the hall?' I suggested, more cheerily than I felt.

Mr Gout gave me a rueful smile. 'Perhaps, my dear. Let us continue.'

Our quest led us up the long gravel driveway. It was lined with spectacularly tall poplar trees on either side, which towered above the heads of the oaks outside the wall and lent a grand feeling to the otherwise rather empty space. Parklands sandwiched the drive, but looked rather drab and dreary in the bleak January light. I thought we might see a deer or two, maybe even a herd, but there was nothing. We did startle a rather sleepy pheasant, who came strutting out of the mist across the path, only to scuttle away as soon as it saw us. The Hall itself, with its grand columns and many windows, slowly grew larger, and more foreboding, as we approached. Directly in front of the Hall was a badly overgrown garden. Brambles, turned hard and brown with the season, choked a series of geometrically shaped beds, rather ruining what someone had presumably designed as an imposing welcome to any of the Hall's approaching guests.

'Are all big houses like this?' I asked. I'd never been to one before. Being born the daughter of a baker, even a successful one, does not tend to give you much cause to be invited to tea by the local gentry.

'Oh, I'd try not to judge too harshly,' Mr Gout said, although his heart wasn't in it. 'I'm sure it's a much more cheery sight in the sunshine. But no, not all of this fine country's ancestral seats are quite so...' he appeared to search for the right word.

'Desolate?' I suggested.

He deflated. 'Well, yes, I suppose so.'

'Have you visited many, during your cases?' I asked.

'One or two, yes. And I had cause to visit a good few more in my youth, of course.'

'Did you? Were...I mean, are...' It was my turn to stumble over my words. I was reminded once again of my master's current predicament. He lived in Oystercatcher Cottage, a property owned by his housekeeper, Mrs Winchester. It was an extremely unusual situation, apparently brought about by the fact that Mr Gout could no longer remember where his own home was. I'd been told this had resulted from some sort of curse, but I knew little more than that and, truthfully, I had been too afraid to ask. I did not know just how far his memory loss went.

'If you are trying to enquire if I come from money, my dear,' he said with a small chuckle that wobbled his chins. 'Then I'm afraid I must disappoint. Any money my family may have had disappeared a very long time ago.'

I was just pondering how that enigmatic

sentence had not actually answered my question when we arrived at the bottom of the Hall's wide front stairs.

'I was rather hoping we would have run into someone by now,' Mr Gout said, looking about the empty grounds in frustration. 'A footman, perhaps, or a maid. I'd settle for a scullery boy at this point!'

'Shall we go around the back?' I suggested.

Mr Gout appeared to think about this. 'No,' he said. 'I think *not*. I don't know about you, but I've had about enough of skulking about in gamekeeper's cottages and wandering deserted grounds like some sort of trespasser. They called us! And I think it's time I threw my rather considerable weight around. We'll go in the front.'

'Is that wise?' I asked. The thought of entering a manor house uninvited, and through the front door no less, did not make me feel good.

'Well,' Mr Gout said, setting his foot upon the bottom stair. 'I think the phrase I'm looking for, my dear – and you'll have to excuse me, but it has been a *most* trying twenty-four hours – is "Bugger it"!' With that he strode confidently up the stairs towards the intimidating wooden doors. I scrambled to keep up with him and had only just alighted on the uppermost step when he was knocking loudly upon the doors with a clenched fist.

'Hello? Anybody home?' he called. Silence. He called again but elicited the same lack of response. 'Disgraceful,' he muttered, shaking his head. 'Very well, they leave us with no choice.'

In the nearest of the doors to us was a large iron ring, which Mr Gout now grabbed and turned. The door creaked open, and we were treated to a view of a darkened hallway that looked every bit as drab as the mist and drizzle we had been walking through. Of life, there was no sign.

'Do you know,' Mr Gout said to me, smoothing back his damp blond hair. 'I'm beginning to get annoyed.'

We entered the hallway, closing the door behind us, and inspected our surroundings. The house, although grand, had a distinctly un-lived-in feel. The walls were lined with a heavy red silk wallpaper that was rather at odds with the Georgian exterior. Dark wooden furniture filled the space before us and there was a central table that held possibly the largest taxidermy fox I had ever seen. It was frozen mid-leap, a vicious snarl on its dusty face, glass eyes dull with age.

I shuddered and Mr Gout made a sound of sympathy. 'How hideous,' he said. 'Although it fits the rest of the welcome we have received at Thicklewood Hall. Where the devil is everyone?'

'What should we do?' I asked, still nervous about being in the grand house uninvited.

'Oh, I dare say if we root about long enough, we'll stumble across someone or other,' Mr Gout said, setting off at a brisk walk in a random direction.

I followed him into what appeared to be a dining room. A long table filled the central part of the floor, fully dressed for what, to my inexperienced eyes, looked like a full banquet. Crystal glasses gleamed, silverware shone, and a large swag of greenery had been placed down the centre of the table, decorated with ribbon and red berries. It was almost cheery, in contrast to the general gloom we had experienced so far.

'Well, *someone* must be in residence at least,' Mr Gout said, examining himself in a gilt-framed mirror that hung above a large ornate fireplace. He tutted at the stubble on his chin and attempted to smooth his hair again.

'Won't we get in trouble?' The sight of the grand table had only increased my feeling of guilt.

'Oh, my dear, have no fear of that! There is not a house in the entire country of Great Britain that I cannot make myself at home in,' Mr Gout said with a dry chuckle. 'Come on.'

We wandered from empty room to empty room. Many were closed up, clearly unused in years. Heavy white sheets were draped across the furniture and they had a damp, dusty smell. Other rooms showed little signs of life. A pipe on a side table that spilled a little fresh tobacco. A jacket, carelessly thrown over the back of a chair and forgotten. One room, some sort of study or library, even had a fire still smouldering in the grate. Shelf after shelf of books, all faded with age, lined the walls. I scanned the two nearest titles: *The Peerage Through the Ages: Volume twenty-seven* and *A Concise Compendium of Gun Dogs*. Hardly riveting stuff. The room did at least feel pleasantly warm, and we found ourselves naturally slowing our explorations as we stretched out chilled fingers in front of the fire.

'Who the bloody hell are you?'

The voice made me jump, and I spun guiltily from the fire to see a pile of dirty clothes in the nearest armchair get to its feet and transform into a middle-aged man. Not literally, of course, although that would not have been the strangest thing I had ever seen. It was just an exceedingly crumpled-looking man. He stared at me blearily. He had several days' worth of dark stubble on his face and his clothes, although fine, looked like they had been upon his person for just as long. A strong smell of liquor wafted from him, making my nose curl and my eyes water.

'I...I'm terribly sorry!' I stuttered. 'We couldn't find anybody at the gates...and, and then there was nobody at the doors either, and...'

'And you thought you'd just stroll right on in uninvited?' the man snarled. 'Bloody cheek! You there! What the devil have you got to say for yourself?' He directed this at Mr Gout, who was still unconcernedly warming himself by the fire, his back to the man.

'And who might you be?' he said over his shoulder.

The dishevelled man's eyes bulged. 'Who am I? *Who am I*? I'm the Earl of York! Who the ruddy hell are you?'

Mr Gout's eyes widened, and his expression

changed, his jaw slackening and falling open. He slapped a meaty hand to his forehead. 'The Earl of York! Of course! Of course! I *knew* there was something familiar about this place. Honestly, I'd forget my own teeth if they weren't fixed into my face. Well, well, the Earl of York.... But no,' he continued pleasantly, turning to face the man at last. 'You are not.'

The man looked ready to explode. 'What? How dare you–'

'The Earl of York must be at least as old as I am, if I have my timelines straight,' Mr Gout continued, still smiling. 'And although you have probably seen better days, I suspect you are not much more than a shade over forty.'

'How *dare you*!' the man blustered, puffing out his chest like an angry robin.

Mr Gout raised an eyebrow. 'How dare I? My good fellow, I am afraid I must direct that very question back at yourself. The sorry state in which we have found what, if I recall correctly, was once the great estate of Thicklewood leaves me to believe that the *real* Earl must be currently incapacitated. For he would never have let it slip into such a sorry situation. I'm guessing that travesty must have occurred on your watch, making you the Earl's son. Am I wrong?'

The man deflated somewhat, but still fixed Mr Gout with an angry glare. 'My father is very ill. I will be Earl soon,' he muttered through clenched teeth.

Mr Gout looked genuinely upset. 'Oh, well, I

am most sorry to hear that. You have my deepest sympathies.'

'Er, thank you,' the man said, looking thoroughly confused. I didn't blame him, as I was struggling to keep up myself. Was Mr Gout saying he *knew* the Earl of York?

Before I could clarify the point, the Earl's son shook himself. 'None of this explains what you are doing trespassing in my study. Geoffrey!' he called, looking about the room as if he expected to see someone. 'Where is that ruddy butler? *Geoffrey!*'

'I'm afraid you are the first person we have seen,' said Mr Gout. 'I admit we feared the entire house had been abandoned…but here you are.'

The Earl's son, assuming that was indeed who the man was, sagged, as if the entire ordeal was becoming too much for him. 'Look, who *are* you?'

Mr Gout beamed, extending a meaty hand towards the man. 'Mr Theophilius Gout, paranormal investigator. This charming young woman here is Clementine Trussel, my apprentice.'

The man's eyes popped again and looked at the hand as if it might bite him. 'Paranormal *what*? Look, is this some sort of joke?'

Mr Gout lowered his hand. 'No joke, my lord. I am afraid there are sinister things afoot in the Thicklewood Estate.'

'What on earth are you drivelling on about?' the man said, then ran a hand across his tired face. 'Good god, maybe I'm hallucinating. Is that it? I knew I shouldn't have had that extra brandy last night.'

'We are quite corporeal, I assure you,' said Mr Gout. 'We were summoned here by letter.'

'Letter? What letter?'

'Sent by your gamekeeper, Mr Harding.'

'*What!*' The man exploded, the effort making him sway slightly. 'That good-for-nothing is inviting crackpots into my home now, is he? Blasted man! Well, you can jolly well bugger off back to wherever you came from, Mr Trout, because Mr Harding had neither the permission nor the authority to summon anyone to *my* estate.'

'*Gout.*'

'What?'

'Mr Gout.'

'Trout, Gout, whatever! Get out!'

'I'm afraid we cannot do that, my lord.'

The man turned a sickly green. '*Geoffrey!*' he roared.

'I feel certain that if your butler were going to attend to you, he would have done so by now. May I suggest you take a seat? You do not appear at all well, my good fellow,' said Mr Gout, gently.

The man did indeed collapse back into his armchair, holding his head in his hands. 'Please, just go away!' he wailed, all bluster leaking out of him.

'Like I say, your grace, I'm afraid we cannot do that. Whether or not he had permission, your gamekeeper summoned me here, and now that I am here, I cannot leave until I have got to the bottom of all this,' said Mr Gout.

'All *what,* for god's sake?' The man did not look up, but buried his head further into his hands.

'The owl, my lord.'

'The wha–' the Earl's son began, then realisation dawned on his face. 'Oh, you can't be bloody serious? That's why you're here? Because of the insane rantings of Mr Harding and that bloody owl of his?'

'His owl?' I asked, struck by the way he said it.

'Yes, his ruddy owl! The man's obsessed with the damn thing!'

'He certainly seems to carry a lot of concern about the creature,' Mr Gout mused.

'Concern?' the man scoffed. 'The whole thing is his own bloody invention! He's off his rocker if you ask me. I'd fire the idiot, only…'

'Only you do not yet have that authority,' Mr Gout surmised.

The man glared at him. 'No. I do not. Yet. But look, take it from me, don't waste your time chasing after that man's personal demons.'

'You think it a hopeless charge, finding the owl?' Mr Gout asked.

'Of course it's hopeless! The damn thing only exists in the man's head. That's the only place you'll find it. Oh, and that wretched statue of his, of course.'

Mr Gout perked up at this. 'What statue might that be?'

'Hasn't he shown you it? You do surprise me. Usually he waves it under the nose of any passing fool stupid enough to let him.'

'He hasn't shown us any such object,' Mr Gout persisted.

'Well, count yourself lucky,' the man spat. 'I wouldn't mind so much if he had any genuine talent, but the thing is barely competent.'

'He created it himself?'

'Whittled it, yes. Seems he has too much time on his hands. No wonder this damnable place is crumbling around our ears.'

'I see,' said Mr Gout. 'And where is this statue?'

'I really couldn't say. Now go away.'

'I have more questions,' said Mr Gout.

The man sunk still further into his chair. The bluster was leaving him by the second, to be replaced with a thick, cloying despair that seeped out of him and hung in a fog across the ceiling.

'What did I do to deserve this?' he asked said ceiling.

Mr Gout smiled with little warmth. 'I wouldn't consider myself qualified to say.'

The man stared at him. 'You really are a very peculiar man, Mr…?'

'Gout.'

'Right, right.' The man looked thoughtful. 'Don't I know a Mr Gout?'

'You do now,' Mr Gout pointed out.

'No, no, I mean…from a long time ago….' He studied my master's face as if hoping for inspiration. Eventually, a small light appeared in his eyes. 'I've got it! Didn't my father go to Oxford with a Gout?'

'We were vaguely acquainted, as I recall,' Mr Gout admitted – reluctantly, it seemed to me. I found myself surprised at the admission. I didn't know why I should be, particularly. Mr Gout was obviously an educated man. I suppose I had not guessed, during those early days of our acquaintance, from what heights he had come. I cannot say precisely why, but the realisation nettled me. Was there *anything* about his life my master had felt the compunction to tell me?

'I knew it!' said the Earl's son, then paused. 'Good lord! Whatever is an Oxford man doing running about the countryside, breaking into country houses and chasing phantoms in the dark? What was it you called yourself? A paranormal investigator? That seems a very odd profession for an Oxbridge man!'

'Well,' said Mr Gout. 'Life can take us in very odd directions, can't it, my lord?'

'That's true enough.'

'But this does not answer my questions,' Mr Gout said, steering the conversation away from his past and back to the matter at hand. 'What else do you know about the owl?'

The man looked blank. 'What else is there to know? It's not real.'

'There, I'm afraid, I must disagree with you. It attacked one of your maids just last night,' said Mr Gout. 'Indeed, I bear proof of the creature's very real nature upon my own person.' He bent his head forward and indicated the scratches he had obtained the night before.

The man looked startled. 'What on earth are you talking about?'

'You did not notice her -- Sally, I believe her name was – being escorted back inside last night by Mr Harding?'

'Last night? Oh, err…no. No, last night I was…' the man trailed off, his eyes slipping to an empty brandy bottle on the table at his side.

'I see,' said Mr Gout. 'Then perhaps my associate and I will take our leave of you after all.'

The man looked distinctly relieved. 'Please do!'

'A pleasure to make your acquaintance,' said Mr Gout. 'Oh, and my sympathies about your father once again. Come on, Miss Trussel, we can show ourselves out.'

With that, he turned around and strode out of the room. His abrupt departure took me a little by surprise, so I was only just beginning to follow by the time he was already disappearing out of the door. To my further surprise, the son of the Earl placed a slightly shaking hand on my arm as I passed.

'Young lady, just exactly how did you become…associated with that man?' he asked.

'I, er…well, he hired me as his assistant,' I mumbled.

The man looked at me strangely. 'There's something about him…' he said. 'Something my father told me, many years ago. I can't seem to quite recall…. Just be careful with him.'

'Mr Gout is a perfect gentleman,' I said stiffly, pulling my arm away.

'No, no, I don't mean like that,' he said. 'There was something else. Some sort of scandal or... oddity,' he finished lamely.

'Well, thank you. I will keep that in mind,' I said. 'Good day, my lord.'

With that I left him and hurried after Mr Gout, who was now some way down the corridor. I glanced back once to find the Earl's son staring after me, scratching the stubble on his chin, a look of deep concern on his face. What had he meant, I wondered?

I turned my attention to the broad back of my master and wondered what he had been like as a college student. It was hard to picture him as anything other than what he was now, somehow. In fact, I found it quite hard to imagine his life before the little cottage in Abermywl, with Mrs Winchester, and this life of supernatural mysteries. I supposed he must have had one. I tried to shake those thoughts from my head. We needed to focus on the case at hand. I caught up to Mr Gout and found his brow deeply furrowed.

'My apologies for the abrupt departure,' he said. 'But I suddenly realised with crystal clarity that the Earl's son there was of no use to us. He clearly has no idea what is happening in his own home. I doubt he pays much attention to anything that isn't going on in his own head. We will have to look elsewhere for our answers.'

'He didn't have much nice to say about Mr Harding,' I said.

Mr Gout snorted. 'No, but then he seems the sort of man who would probably not have much nice to say about anyone, especially those of a lower class than himself. Then again, as we have discovered for ourselves, Mr Harding is a challenging man to recommend the company of to anyone.'

'You don't think this whole thing is just in his head, do you?'

'I might be tempted to that line of reasoning,' Mr Gout admitted. 'If it were not for what we witnessed last night. We saw the owl attack that poor maid. And I know a revenant when I see one. No. Mr Hasting may indeed be mad, but that doesn't mean that there isn't something deeply wrong here in Thicklewood.'

'So…have you been here before? To Thicklewood?' I couldn't resist asking the question. But he shook his head.

'No. But there was something about the name…it's been bothering me ever since we received Mr Harding's letter. Some memory of a memory, in the back of my head. Now I know what it was. I did indeed know that man's father, many years ago.'

'Were you friends?'

Mr Gout made a face. But all he said was, 'It was another life, my dear,' before lapsing into another thoughtful silence.

'What do we do now?' I asked eventually, when it was clear he would not be drawn further.

I didn't much fancy wandering around the empty house all morning. It was giving me the creeps.

'What we should have done on arrival,' said Mr Gout. 'We must interview someone with a little sense. We shall seek out the servants' quarters, my dear. I wish to speak with the maid Sally anyway, and see how she is faring after her ordeal last night.'

It didn't take us long to find the flight of stairs that led down to the lower floors. This was where the many servants that made a large estate like Thicklewood Hall run smoothly dwelt. I was less than surprised to find the corridors empty. It was much less grand below stairs. The stairs themselves were of unadorned wood. The walls were plain whitewashed plaster. A faint smell of mildew hung in the air, and when I touched one wall, it was damp and a little tacky. I supposed the Earl and his family saw no reason to spend on a part of the house their rich friends would never see.

Although the servants' quarters had initially seemed just as empty as the house above it, we did eventually hear the sounds of activity coming from somewhere in the warren of whitewashed corridors. We followed the hum of distant conversation, the temperature of the dank corridors warming as we went, and at length arrived in a large, high-ceilinged room that could only be a kitchen. We were hit by a damp heat that rolled over my face, making me blink. It smelt of boiled vegetables. Once my eyes had cleared, they were drawn to the source of the heat: the largest cast iron range I had ever seen. It seemed to fill one wall, black and hulking. It belched smoke and steam in equal measure, which rolled up the walls and condensed on the ceiling, creating an almost unbearably humid atmosphere. A cluster of copper pots and pans bubbled away. Opposite was an equally huge dresser, which must have held enough fine china to furnish a banquet. Between the stove and dresser stood a long, worn wooden table, at which sat five very surprised servants.

One was a stout yet formidable woman, who, if she were not the head cook, had clearly missed her calling in life. She had a round, rosy-cheeked face that sagged at the jowls, and fierce blue eye that regarded us with suspicion. She frowned and opened her mouth, but Mr Gout beat her to the punch. Bowing grandly, he beamed his most winning smile at her.

'Good morrow. Allow me to introduce myself! My name is Mr Gout and this charming young lady is my associate, Miss Trussel. We have been visiting with the Earl's son.'

This was stretching the truth a little, I felt, but it seemed to have the desired effect. The cook closed her mouth and appeared to reconsider her first words.

'Good morning to you,' she eventually said. 'How may we be of assistance?'

The other servants fidgeted nervously, clearly unsure what was expected of them and exactly what manner of guests we were. I did my best to look as though I had every right to be standing uninvited in the kitchen of a country estate.

Mr Gout continued to smile warmly. 'We are here on a rather delicate matter. I wonder if we might be able to take up a little of the butler's valuable time, or whomsoever else might be in a position to help us?'

The cook's lips thinned, and her face took on an unreadable expression. 'I'm afraid Mr Perkins is… indisposed. I'm Mrs Jones, the head cook. Perhaps I might be of assistance?'

'I'm sure that would be quite adequate, Mrs Jones. Indeed, it would be an absolute pleasure to share a little tea with you. I'm afraid to say we quite missed breakfast.'

'Er…right, certainly. Yes, tea,' said the cook, allowing only the merest trembling of an eyebrow and motioning to one of the other servants, who scuttled off towards a large copper kettle resting on one side of the range. Mrs Jones shot looks at the remaining servants, who quickly made themselves scarce. 'Will you be comfortable enough at the table here, or…?' she asked, letting the question hang in the air.

'Oh, most comfortable indeed, Mrs Jones! Why, what could be more comfortable than sitting in such a delicious-smelling kitchen?'

My jaw threatened to drop open at that, but I caught it at the last second.

'I can see you run a tight ship. Very organised, I'm sure,' he continued. 'Why, I expect you have a little something put aside, don't you, for when visitors might drop in unexpectedly? A little cake perhaps? A biscuit or two?'

Mrs Jones took the hint, although her lips thinned yet further, making her mouth a thin sliver across her face. The remaining servant set down three cups of tea on the large wooden table and was sent scurrying off to retrieve a large cake tin from the very top shelf of the dresser. The ladder required for the job swayed alarmingly, but the servant seemed well used to the task and was dishing out thick slices of fruit cake in no time.

'Please, do take a seat, both of you.' Mrs Jones motioned to two of the empty chairs, taking one for herself.

'How delightful!' said Mr Gout, taking a seat and immediately reaching for the largest slice of cake, even though it meant taking it from the place set out for Mrs Jones. The cook noted the action, but said nothing.

Once we were all seated, I took a small sip of tea and felt the need to say something. 'This is really very kind of you.'

The cook smiled at me thinly, her keen eyes taking in, I'm sure, my youth, and trying to work out my relationship to Mr Gout. 'Perhaps you could explain what this is all about?'

'Certainly, my good woman,' said Mr Gout, swallowing the last of his cake. He reached for mine, then remembered himself enough to slip me a surreptitious look. I nodded with a small smile and with a grin of gratitude he took it, replacing it with his empty plate. 'We are here at the bequest of the gamekeeper, Mr Harding.'

Mrs Jones looked surprised. 'Mr Harding? I thought you said you were visiting with his lordship?'

'Oh, we just had a very revealing chat,' Mr Gout said through a mouthful of my cake. 'But I'm afraid he was in no, ahem…condition to provide us with the information we require.'

'I see,' said the cook, her eyebrows knitting together, her lips so thin now they were practically disappearing. 'And for what reason, exactly, did Mr Harding summon you here?'

'As I said, it is a delicate matter. I wonder if Mr Harding has perhaps mentioned anything to you about a certain…owl?'

Mr Gout asked innocently enough, but I saw the slight shift in his demeanour, the way his eyes focused more sharply on the cook. As it was, he need not have been examining her so closely to spot her immediate reaction to the mention of the owl. She almost dropped her cup of tea, spilling a goodly portion of it upon the table. Her ruddy face paled until the only spots of colour left were two red splotches on her cheeks. She set her cup down and, staring at us fearfully, asked, 'What do you know of the White Owl?'

Mr Gout pushed the plate that now contained the remaining crumbs of my cake away from him, taking a sip of tea as he did so. He then put down his own cup and, with all traces of the pleasant, jolly visitor gone from his face, looked at the cook with his full attention.

'I see we can dispense with any games,' he said. 'We are here about the owl that haunts the woods of this estate.'

The cook's hands shook. 'I…I knew Mr Harding had written to someone…or at least he said he had. I didn't know what to believe…but here you are.'

'Here I am.' Mr Gout offered her a small, reassuring smile.

'How…' Mrs Jones gulped, steadying herself. 'How can I help?'

'You can answer one very simple question for me,' said Mr Gout. 'A question that I am sad to say Mr Harding refused. Who died, Mrs Jones?'

The cook, who had seemed so formidable when we first entered the kitchen, seemed to crumble at the question. She put a shaking hand to her mouth and her shoulders trembled.

'It was terrible,' she said. 'Oh god, how I wish I could forget that day. There are some memories that no soul should have to live with.'

Mr Gout got to his feet, fetched the teapot from where the servant had left it on the side, returned to the table and refilled the cook's cup. He handed it back to her with a smile. 'It's alright, my dear. We are here to help.'

'But Mr Harding…' she said, gulping in big lungfuls of breath as though she were about to cry.

'We owe no allegiance to Mr Harding,' Mr Gout said. 'He may have been the one to summon us here, but now that we are, our priority is to see this case to its conclusion for the benefit of all wronged parties.'

The cook looked deep into his eyes. She seemed to search for something. Perhaps some sense of whether he was genuine. Whatever it was, she obviously felt she found it.

'His name was Thomas,' she said, her voice hardly above a whisper. 'Thomas Harding.'

Mr Gout's eyebrows rose up his forehead and I couldn't help but blurt out, 'They were related? The man who died and Mr Harding? The gamekeeper Mr Harding, I mean.'

The cook nodded miserably. 'They were brothers. Thomas was the head gardener, Terence, the gamekeeper. Both of them have worked… *had* worked here since they were boys. Practically brought up on the estate .' She paused, apparently unsure of how to continue.

'It's alright,' Mr Gout prompted, putting a gentle hand on her shoulder. 'In your own time.'

'Oh sir! It was just dreadful what happened to Thomas. Dreadful!' Mrs Jones wailed, letting the tears fall from her eyes at last. 'And he was a good man. A fine man. He did not deserve to go like that, and when he was engaged to be married too!' She put down her tea, untouched, and rooted around in the sleeve of her smock until she produced a hanky, which she noisily blew her nose into. This seemed to settle her a little, and after a few deep breaths she spoke again, calmer now.

'It was me who found him, in the forest. Almost eighteen months ago now. I went out one morning, just as I often do…did, to collect mushrooms – there's a good spot, sir, in the heart of the woodland. It's a bit of a walk, but worth it. Best mushrooms for miles around. Anyway, as I say, I went out, just like normal, but when I got there… well, there was Thomas. Dead, sir.' She stopped speaking again and shivered. Mr Gout gave her shoulder another encouraging squeeze.

She took a deep breath. 'He'd been horribly mutilated, sir. Whoever…or *whatever* killed him…. Look, I'm a woman of the world, Mr Gout. I've seen a thing or two in my life. But this…'

'I am most terribly sorry to make you relive it,' said Mr Gout, his face solemn. 'If it were not of the utmost importance, I would certainly spare you the pain.'

The cook sniffed and nodded. 'It was a violent attack. That's all I can say. That, and poor Thomas had obviously been there some time before I happened upon him. The animals…well, I'm sure I don't have to describe it to you.'

Mr Gout nodded, releasing her shoulder and sitting back down in his seat next to mine. 'Indeed not, my good woman. I thank you. That cannot have been easy.'

Mrs Jones sighed. 'To tell the truth, I have done everything I can to block that day from my memory. Poor, *poor* Thomas. He was a well-liked man, Mr Gout. Unlike his brother.' Here she scowled in distaste.

'Mr Harding does seem...a difficult man,' I said hesitantly.

The cook gave a bark of bitter laughter. 'That's the polite way of putting it,' she said. 'Yet he and Thomas had always been close. I guess there are some things only a relative can love.' She shrugged. 'But even Thomas fell out with him in the end.'

'They had an argument, the two brothers?' Mr Gout asked, leaning forward in his chair.

Mrs Jones looked at him shrewdly. 'They did. And believe me, there was more than one of us who wondered...but there was never any proof. And besides, it seems hard to believe even a man as disagreeable as Mr Harding would...*could* do that to his own blood.'

She sighed again. It was obvious the affair weighed heavily on her heart.

'And there is poor Sally,' she continued. 'Bless her young soul. To lose the man you love so young... life can be cruel.'

'Wait, it was the maid Sally who was engaged to Thomas?' I asked.

The cook nodded. 'Indeed, poor girl. I'm not sure she's really gotten over it.'

'That reminds me,' said Mr Gout. 'How is the poor girl?'

The cook looked confused. 'Who?'

'Sally. Her wounds were not too deep, but nevertheless it must have been a nasty shock for her.'

Mrs Jones looked horrified. 'Wounds? What do you mean? When was Sally injured?'

I felt a sinking feeling in my stomach, and it was now Mr Gout's turn to look confused.

'Why, last night, of course. The owl, it...' he paused, and I could see an unpleasant thought was taking root in his head. 'Mrs Jones,' he said, his face intense. 'Am I to understand that Mr Harding did not return here last night with Sally?'

The cook was looking completely nonplussed. 'No,' she said. 'I haven't seen Sally since yesterday evening. She didn't turn up for work this morning. I said nothing to the master because...well, to be honest it's not the first time, and, after Thomas...' she paused here, shooting Mr Gout a slightly fearful look, but he waved away the admission and she continued. 'Perhaps I'm too soft on her. Anyway, I haven't seen Mr Harding since...it must be at least yesterday morning. He keeps himself to himself, mostly. What's going on!'

Mr Gout had got to his feet, and the cook was looking scared.

'I am not entirely sure of that myself, Mrs Jones, but I fear young Sally may be in grave danger.'

Mrs Jones got to her feet, knocking back her chair in her hurry, one hand flying to her mouth in horror.

'Last night, not long after our arrival at Thicklewood Hall estate, the so-called White Owl attacked us outside Mr Harding's cottage,' said Mr

Gout. 'We fled to the safety of his cottage, but then Miss Sally appeared. A scuffle ensued and poor Sally's face was badly scratched by the bird. I tried to offer my assistance, but Mr Harding was insistent that she be brought back to the hall. He left in our wagon to do just that and returned later in the evening. He shortly left again, claiming that, as we were planning on staying the night, he would have to find quarters in the main house. He did not return this morning. I saw nothing suspicious in that at first, but now I am beginning to fear that nothing occurred last night as we were led to believe.'

The cook shook her head, all colour gone from her face. 'He never came here,' she said. 'And I've seen no wagon either. Oh, poor Sally! What is that man up to?'

'And it is not possible that this could have happened without your notice?' Mr Gout asked.

She shook her head again. 'Not possible. What with the master being...well, being the way he is, and Mr Perkins is no better. No, nothing happens at Thicklewood without my knowing about it...well, normally at any rate.'

'Then I think you should rouse the household and begin a search for Sally and Mr Harding at once,' said Mr Gout.

Mrs Jones wrung her hands, ran to the door, paused, then trotted back. 'I don't understand,' she said. 'Is...is it Mr Harding who's taken her? Or the owl? I don't understand what's happening.'

'Neither do I, Mrs Jones. Not yet,' said Mr Gout.

'But I think I can start to guess. However, I will not share those guesses until there is proper evidence. For the time being, we know that both Mr Harding and young Sally are missing, and that current evidence would suggest that Mr Harding has taken her without her consent. Do you need help to rally the household?' he prompted, when the cook still did not move.

She appeared to pull herself together. 'No. No, I can do it.'

With that, she hurried from the room, crying out names at the top of her voice. We heard the hurried footsteps of the servants, rallying to her cries.

Alone in the kitchen, I met Mr Gout's eyes. 'I'm confused.' I admitted. 'I thought we were here to deal with the owl. Now it seems more likely we need to deal with Mr Harding!'

My master looked grave. 'I fear we have been played for fools, my dear Clementine. I only hope we have not delayed too long. For Sally's sake.'

PART FOUR

The rousing of the household turned out to be an eye-opening affair. By rights such a thing should have been overseen by the butler, the head of the house when it came to all matters below stairs. However, the as-yet-unseen Mr Perkins took some considerable time to be winkled out of his personal parlour by Mrs Jones, leaving the rest of the staff to work themselves up into quite the fizz.

Maids marauded through the corridors, shrieking Sally's name as loud as their young lungs could manage, pulling back curtains and flinging open cupboards in the vain hope of finding the missing girl stashed inside. Footmen marched up and down, wearing holes in the thin rugs, beating their puffed-up chests with tightly clenched fists, and proclaiming loudly what they would do to the dastardly Harding should he show his cowardly face in the Hall again. When Mr Perkins finally staggered into the main hallway, heavily supported by the head cook, his quavering appeals for calm were summarily ignored and he was nearly bowled over by a particularly frantic-looking woman brandishing a mop like a weapon of war. The butler was a beanpole of a man, with hollow cheeks and a rough, red nose that spoke of his obvious affinity with the bottle. He looked around the hallway at the rushing bodies of his staff, his mouth flapping open and closed.

Throughout all this, Mr Gout had remained uncharacteristically apart. He had made no attempt to intercede with the staff, instead standing by a large bay window, staring out at the ruined gardens beyond with a worried, distant expression. I stood by his side, feeling utterly useless. At the butler's ineffectual arrival I decided I could remain silent no longer.

'Should we not do something to help?'

Mr Gout turned his head slightly at the sound of my voice, but his eyes remained locked on some point in the distance. 'What's that, my dear?'

'I said, should we not do something to help, Mr Gout? We will never find Sally and Mr Harding at this rate.'

But I was already losing him.

'I must think…' he mumbled, head turning away again.

Then, quite unexpectedly, my temper snapped.

'For goodness' sake, Mr Gout, are we here to help these people or to stare uselessly out of the window?'

The words escaped my mouth before I could

clamp my teeth down upon them. The irritations of the last few days bubbled up all at once, but, just like the froth on a pan that is boiling over, my anger fizzled to nothing as it hit the open air. My outburst had at least succeeded in gaining my master's full attention, but now I looked at his surprised face with horror, a burning shame already creeping across my cheeks.

'I...I'm so sorry, Mr Gout. I... I didn't mean to... that is to say...'

But Mr Gout put out a hand to silence me.

'Do not say another word,' he said. 'You are quite right, my dearest Clementine. It is I who must apologise. I find I am not myself.'

'Is it...is it because of the other revenant?' I asked. 'The one you came across before?'

Then Mr Gout smiled at me. It was quite unlike any smile I had seen on his round face before. Normally, his eyes would twinkle, the corners of his mouth tugging upwards in an almost irrepressible joy. His cheeks would crease and bulge, his teeth flashing in genuine amusement. But this was not a happy smile. I think it might just have been the saddest expression I had even seen.

'You are a very perceptive young woman, Miss Trussel,' he said. 'Yes. I find my thoughts are drawn to events of the past, and try as I might, I dwell on them like an old fool. Forgive me.'

'Do you want to talk about it?' I offered, a slight panic awaking inside me at the thought of trying to offer a man such as Mr Gout words of wisdom or comfort. But to my simultaneous disappointment and relief, he shook his head.

'You were quite right in your admonishments, my dear. Now is not the time. Later…perhaps.'

Then the spell was broken, and he turned to face the chaos taking place in the rest of the room. His swift eyes took in the panicking servants, the ineffectual butler, and the exasperated Mrs Jones with a single sweep of the room.

'Mrs Jones!' he called to the cook. 'Might I suggest you allow Mr Perkins there to take a seat? He looks exhausted.'

Taking the hint immediately, the sturdy cook practically dropped the unfortunate Mr Perkins into the nearest chair, not giving him a second look. She then bawled out orders in his stead like a sergeant major.

'Phillipa, Geraldine, stop squawking like a pair of old jackdaws and go search the top floor. Master Samuel, instead of standing there like a hen with a toothache, take Josiah and search the cellar. Mrs Wetwhistle, do put that mop down. There's a good woman! Now, find that sister of yours and get yourselves to the first floor.'

Within seconds, order was regained. I was impressed.

Mr Perkins, for his part, did his best to stay sitting upright and looking important.

It was at this point that the master of the house, presumably shaken from his private den of iniquity by the many raised voices, made an appearance.

'What in the seven hells is going on?' he cried. 'Geoffrey! What is the meaning of this?'

It was unfortunate for Mr Perkins that at that moment he lost his battle of wills with the chair and began a slow slide out of one side to the floor.

The Earl's son looked apoplectic, his face a dangerous-looking rouge. '*What is happening*?' he demanded again.

Mrs Jones hesitated, uncertain. But this time, Mr Gout was alert and ready.

'Ah, your lordship. Just in time. Allow me to explain...'

This, I thought to myself, *will have to be good!*

Half an hour later, the entire mansion had been searched with no sign of either missing person. This included the time it took to explain to the irate Earl's son exactly what was going on. He had been at first disbelieving, and then frankly disinterested. Mr Gout and I had now joined the servants as their search extended to the grounds. While others combed the parklands within the Hall's walls, Mrs Jones, Mr Gout and I made our way back to the gamekeeper's cottage to begin a search of the woodlands. I did not know how far the woods stretched from the house, but it seemed an almost impossible task. As we approached the little house, Mrs Jones, whose initial fear had turned to a steely determination to find her missing charge, turned to me, whilst Mr Gout was busy searching a nearby copse.

'Tell me, what exactly is the nature of Mr Gout's business?'

I decided that truth was the best response. 'He is a paranormal investigator.'

I was impressed by how little the woman reacted. 'And you are?' she asked.

'I'm his apprentice.'

'My dear girl, how on earth did you end up...' she trailed off.

'The short version? Something tried to eat my grandmother, and he stopped it,' I said with a shrug.

This time, the surprise did register on the old cook's face. 'Well...I suppose it is a good thing that both of you are here, then.'

'I'm afraid it seems we've been of little help so far,' I admitted.

'Just so I have this straight in my head,' said the cook. 'Mr Harding summoned you here to deal with the owl?'

'In a manner of speaking. His letter didn't mention the exact nature of the problem, just that the estate needed my master's help.'

'Curious,' said the cook. 'What is he up to? And what *is* the owl?'

I paused before answering, for ideas about that had been forming in my head ever since our discussion around the kitchen table. I was a little afraid of how the cook might react. 'Mr Gout says it's a revenant, a vengeful spirit. Someone who has died in tragic circumstances.'

I watched her face carefully, but Mrs Jones merely looked thoughtful. Then her eyes set with certainty. 'Thomas,' she said.

'That would be the logical conclusion.' This came from Mr Gout, who had exhausted his search of the nearby trees and rejoined us on the path.

'But…but how exactly? Why would he come back like…like that? And why would he attack Sally? He loved her!'

Mr Gout looked as though he were picking his words carefully. 'A revenant is made when a soul cannot find peace because of some great injustice or betrayal. The manner of Thomas's death, as you have described, certainly seems to fit the bill. Obviously, I do not know the particular details.'

'But why the owl?' Mrs Jones said with a shudder. 'Poor Thomas was such a jolly soul. I just can't picture that creepy thing being him.'

Mr Gout looked grim. 'It isn't – not as you remember him, at any rate. His soul has been twisted and warped by what happened. It's had eighteen months to dwell on all that darkness, unable to move on or find rest. Fixating on the wrong done to him. It's no wonder he focused his haunting on his brother. But what I can't quite fathom is the significance of the owl. He would only take that shape if it held some powerful emotion or symbol for him. As yet I am unsure of what that could be.'

'That I might be able to answer,' said Mrs Jones. 'Thomas loved owls.'

Mr Gout shook his head. 'No, no. It wouldn't be because he loved something. It has to hold negative connotations.'

The old cook tutted. 'I'm getting to that,' she said. 'He also loved carving and whittling things from wood. His brother did, too. In fact, it was something they often did together. After Sally and Thomas announced their engagement, he worked with his brother to make a carving as a wedding gift for Sally. It was an owl. Of course, then the brothers fell out and I don't know what happened to it after that.'

'Interesting,' said Mr Gout.

'That would seem a powerful reason for his soul to focus on an owl,' I said. 'Especially if it was his brother who killed him.'

Mrs Jones took a deep breath. 'I still find it hard to believe that he would do something like that to anyone, let alone his own brother!'

By this point, we had reached the edge of the woodland by the stone cottage where we had first seen the owl the night before. I felt another shiver as I looked up into the branches. It was full daylight, only a little past noon, and the sun was streaming strongly through from above. The mist of the early morning had been burnt away and yet I could not escape the feeling of menace that had pervaded that area ever since our arrival the night before. The menagerie of wooden figures in front of the cottage didn't help. I almost felt they might come alive at any moment. An army of rotting creatures.

'Does...does anyone else feel that?' I asked, feeling a little silly. But Mrs Jones nodded solemnly.

'Oh, yes. I feel it alright. There's been this...this sort of growing sense of doom...that's the only way I can think of to describe it. It's saturated the whole woodland for weeks now. Not that I come out here much these days. Not since...' the woman shivered.

'You don't come to pick mushrooms anymore?' I asked.

I could actually see the cook's skin turn a little green in the sunlight. 'I find I have lost my taste for them,' she said.

'But what of your master, the Earl's son? Surely he still requires them from time to time?' asked Mr Gout.

The cook gave a rueful laugh. 'I don't know if you've noticed it, sir, but the Earl's son is not very interested in a breakfast that does not come in a bottle. Quite frankly, there is little point even serving him meals. He barely touches what I give him, let alone comment on its lack of mushrooms.'

'I had noticed,' said Mr Gout, stroking his stubbly chin thoughtfully. 'In fact, if you will forgive me, Mrs Jones, I have noticed a great deal that is unusual about the running of Thicklewood Hall.'

The cook gave another bark of laughter. It sounded bitter. 'You're not wrong.'

'For example, where are the rest of the family? We were given to understand that the Earl is gravely ill. Are they all housed elsewhere with him?'

She nodded. 'In London, or so we hear. The

truth is, Mr Gout, we have not seen any of them here for years. The Earl's son comes back for a month here or there, supposedly to check up on the place, but he spends the entire time staring at the bottom of a bottle.'

'And do you know what ails his father?'

'Old age, as far as I know,' she said with a shrug. 'He must be in his eighties by now. I should be so lucky to live as long! But none of this is finding poor Sally.'

'No, indeed not,' Mr Gout agreed, transferring his attention to the mass of trees. 'You have us at a disadvantage here, Mrs Jones. How would you suggest to best search the woods?'

We made a thorough search of the cottage and its immediate surroundings, during which I sorted through the carved wooden animals in search of an owl, but found none. We awaited the arrival of reinforcements and then split into groups of two, combing the area directly around the span of the estate walls and working outwards. I found myself partnered with the cook, and it was we, after barely more than half an hour of searching, who found the first clue. Our wagon. The one Mr Gout and I had arrived in.

We found it resting deep in a patch of brambles. Mr Harding had obviously pushed it in to hide it as best he could. The wagon seemed intact, but there was no sign of our poor horse. It had obviously been there at some point, because there were clear hoofprints in the more churned-up ground, and a pile of droppings near a tree close to where the wagon was hidden.

'He must have left our horse here with the wagon when he came back to the cottage last night, then gone back for it later,' I surmised.

'But why did he come back to the cottage at all?' asked the cook. 'If his true goal in all this was to kidnap poor Sally, why take that risk?'

I had been thinking about this. 'He was very agitated that we had taken longer to arrive than he expected. I think he planned the whole thing, but he'd expected to have more time with us to get his story straight. The only thing I can't quite figure out is why Sally was there in the first place. If, like you say, there was no real love lost between them, then why was she going to his cottage at that time of night? Especially given how the owl seems to have been common knowledge.'

'She always took Mr Harding his dinner at about that time,' said Mrs Jones.

'But he shouted at her that he'd told her *not* to.'

The cook nodded. 'He did. More than a week ago. He told her the owl made it too dangerous.'

'Then why did she go last night?'

'Oh, I just can't make head nor tails of it, I really can't!' cried the cook, throwing her hands up in the air.

'And what role were Mr Gout and myself to play?' I mused, almost to myself. But I could make no sense of it, and resolved to return my full attention to the task at hand.

I looked again at the ground where our horse's hoofprints could clearly be seen. It looked as if he had been tied to a tree, most likely whilst Mr Hasting left to return to the cottage. Then I noticed that there were more prints, leading away from the tree and off into the undergrowth.

'Look, there's a trail,' I said. 'Maybe we can follow it.'

'In all this?' Mrs Jones sounded doubtful. But now I had my eye in I could clearly see the horse's trail and I led the way, the cook following silently behind me. We walked for about ten minutes like that; me with my nose to the ground like a bloodhound, Mrs Jones following behind, grumbling about the mud and the brambles that scratched at us. We reached some stony ground, and I thought I'd lost the trail after all, but I picked it back up and we continued.

'Are you sure this is wise?' Mrs Jones said after a few more minutes. 'What if we do find Mr Harding? What if he gets violent? I'd feel a lot happier if we had that stout master of yours with us – no offence.'

'None taken,' I mumbled, intent on my task, but suddenly wondering if she was right. Perhaps it would be best to return and wait till we had more back-up.

In the end, it did not matter. We entered a small clearing and there, slumped up against a tree, was Mr Harding.

Quite, quite dead.

PART FIVE

Mrs Jones' scream rang out like the cry of a startled woodland beast. It, more than the discovery of the corpse, made my heart skip a beat.

'What…what's happened to him?' she screeched at me. 'Oh, heavens above! He's been attacked, he's been…. First Thomas and now his brother. Am I cursed to forever more be stumbling across bodies in these accursed woods?'

I could forgive her consternation. Mr Harding made for a grisly sight. He was covered in gashes and cuts, his clothes red with his blood, the ground beneath him dark where it had seeped into the soil. I put my hand to my mouth, a wave of nausea rising up my gullet. My mind raced. Who had done this? Or what?

A sudden noise made us both jump, and Mrs Jones let out another squawk of alarm. My heart lurched again as I spotted a shadowy movement through the trees. I sucked in a relieved breath when

I realised it was just our horse. Not sure what else to do, I went to fetch it. I gave the body a wide berth, approaching the startled animal slowly.

'It's alright, boy,' I said. 'It's just me. You remember me, don't you?'

The beast was clearly alarmed, but seemed to recognise me and settled a little, allowing me to get hold of its bridle.

'That's a good boy. It's alright,' I said, stroking its thick neck. It flared its nostrils at me in response, but allowed me to lead it back to the clearing. I avoided the body once again.

'Your horse, I presume?' Mrs Jones said as we approached.

I nodded. 'Looks like Mr Hasting had quite a long trip planned.' I indicated the saddlebags that were still flung over the horse's flanks.

'Then he must have had Sally with him!' The cook looked around the clearing as if she expected the girl to jump out of one of the bushes at any moment. She stilled as a further thought hit her. 'Unless…unless he already…' Her eyes widened, filling with tears as the terrible thought hit home.

'We still have no evidence to suggest that Sally has been harmed,' I pointed out quickly. 'We don't even know if she was here yet. I suggest we…er, examine the scene.'

The cook looked horrified. 'I'm not going anywhere near that!' she pointed at the pale, bloody figure against the tree. 'Besides, shouldn't we get out of here? It might not be safe.'

'You don't have to,' I said. 'You keep a lookout while I see what I can find. We should try to find out if Sally was here or not. It might help us find her.'

I began searching the ground of the clearing whilst Mrs Jones kept a nervous eye out for anybody approaching. In truth, I was just as nervous as her. I was doing my best to appear otherwise, but I was not yet used to being in the presence of a dead body. I tried to keep my eyes averted from Mr Harding as I searched for any sign that Sally had been in the clearing. There was an old, rusted garden incinerator placed in the centre of the clearing. It was cold, but full of ash. Mr Harding had clearly been burning something. I took a stick and disturbed the pale grey fragments, which puffed up into the air, catching in my throat and making me cough. The stick hit against something solid and, with a bit of digging, I pulled a wooden lump out of the metal container. At first I thought it was just a piece of firewood. I was about to drop it back in when the carved shape of feathers, poking out through the soot and ash, caught my eye. A hurried dust and a wiping on the wet grass confirmed it. It was an owl.

'What's that you've got there?' Mrs Jones came over, and I showed her what I'd found.

'The owl,' she said, tears welling again in her eyes. 'I didn't realise he'd kept the thing. It should have gone to Sally, really.'

'But why? What was he carrying it around with him for? And why stop to burn the thing if he was trying to make a getaway? I don't understand this at all.'

'I do not know. But it doesn't tell us if Sally was here,' the cook said, moving away.

I thought I wouldn't have long until her anxiety won out and she demanded we leave and seek reinforcements. I got back to scanning the ground. After a few minutes, I still had found nothing that might have indicated Sally's presence. There was only one place left to look. I really didn't want to.

I forced myself to face the corpse of Mr Harding. It was not a pleasant sight. I tried not to think too hard about what had caused his many injuries, but the picture of the white owl's razor-sharp talons kept clawing themselves into my mind. But Mr Harding's wounds looked too large, too deep. I felt a thrill of terror at the thought of something larger out there in the trees. I decided Mrs Jones was right. It wasn't safe to stay here. We needed to take the poor horse back and bring reinforcements. I was just about to turn and tell her so, when something in the dead gamekeeper's hand caught my eye. It was a lock of pale blonde hair.

About an hour later, we returned to the scene with Mr Gout and a couple of the larger servants in tow. I watched as my master surveyed the scene, taking everything in.

'Well,' he said. 'It would seem we have failed Mr Harding. I am sorry for it.'

'But he's a kidnapper and a murderer!' said Mrs

Jones.

Mr Gout gave her a reproving look. 'We do not know that for sure. There may have been hope for him yet. Now we will never know.'

The cook looked unconvinced. 'Well, right now I'm more concerned about finding Sally.'

'Of course.' Mr Gout dropped to his knees and retrieved the wooden carving from where I had left it in the grass. 'The first thing that strikes me is that Mr Harding clearly knew a lot more about his persecutor than he let on.'

'Why do you say that?' I asked.

He indicated the owl. 'He tried to burn this. That shows me he knew both who the owl was, and *what* it was. He must have figured out the connection between the owl and this statue. Which meant that he must have done his supernatural homework.'

'I don't understand,' said Mrs Jones.

'It is no simple coincidence he tried to destroy this as he prepared to flee,' Mr Gout said. 'He must have learnt that revenants are tethered to a particular place or object. Once he'd learnt that, it can't have been too hard to figure out it was the statue, given the form his brother had taken. Unfortunately for him, he didn't do his homework quite thoroughly enough. Destroying the object tethering his brother would indeed have dispelled him to the next world, but he failed to take into account that any damage to the object would also draw his brother to him.'

'So it was Thomas who...who did this to him?' Mrs Jones gulped.

'I am certain of it.'

'But how would he have known any of this?' I asked. 'It's not exactly common knowledge.'

'That is certainly the question,' said Mr Gout, scratching his pink chin thoughtfully. 'I should have realised that he knew more than he claimed. This whole situation has been peculiar from the start. Summoning me here without permission. Expecting us to deal with the creature within moments of our arrival. It is clear he summoned us here purely as pawns in some larger game of his. Unfortunately for him, he rather overestimated his expertise.'

'But what do we do now? Thomas...the owl, whatever it is, has Sally. We need to find them!' said Mrs Jones.

'Well, we have the answer to half of that right here.' Mr Gout held up the charred statue.

'You mean try to burn the statue again?' I said. 'But won't–'

'It will bring the owl to us, yes.'

'That...doesn't seem like a brilliant plan.'

'I'm still finding it hard to believe that Thomas would do something like that,' said Mrs Jones, shooting a brief but horrified look at the body, still lying at the base of the tree. 'He was a good man. Whatever his brother might have been. Thomas never hurt a soul.'

Mr Gout looked grave. 'I would remind you

that you said similar of Terence Harding, not that long ago. Besides, we are not dealing with the Thomas you knew, Mrs Jones. He, I am afraid to say, is dead and gone. A vengeful spirit is not the exact person who died, it is more of a separate entity that has grown out of the tortured soul of the deceased. It is Thomas, yes, but it is also more like a wild beast. Run by its basest instincts. In this case, I believe those instincts are to protect Sally, most notably from his own brother. Given recent events, it does not seem too far of a stretch to suppose that their falling out before his death was linked to his brother's interest in his fiancé.'

Mrs Jones shook her head. 'But then why take her? If he'd killed his brother, then surely Sally was safe?'

'He will not see it that way. He eliminated one threat, yes. But the entire world is a threat if you look at something with such blinkered vision. We have a further problem, however.'

'What?' I asked.

'This form that Thomas has become…it is not a natural state of being, so it is not sustainable, certainly not stable.'

'What are you saying?'

Mr Gout sighed. He looked troubled. 'You must understand that creatures such as this are not common. It is not as if every fifth person who dies comes back as a revenant. Reports and documented accounts of dealing with such creatures are rarer still. But the ones that do exist all agree on one thing. The longer the creature is around, the more aggressive it becomes.'

'Well, we've seen that,' I said. 'Mr Harding himself said that the owl started off just watching, before it started attacking.'

'Precisely. And if we can rely on Mr Harding's timeline as accurate, then that means that Thomas has been in this form for some weeks. He will be reaching boiling point by now.'

'But what does all this *mean*?' said Mrs Jones.

'It means that by now any sense of who he was will have left Thomas. By now, he will just be a mass of emotion. That makes him unpredictable.'

'Are you saying he could hurt Sally?'

'If we do not find her in time? That is a real possibility, yes.'

'Well then, we must find her at once!' the cook cried.

'But we can't just repeat what Mr Harding did,' I objected again. 'Unless we want to end up the same way?'

'Ah, but we have an advantage,' said Mr Gout.

'What's that?'

'I've done this before.'

'I thought you said these things were rare?' said Mrs Jones.

'Incredibly.'

'And yet you just happened to have dealt with one before?' Mrs Jones' eyes narrowed suspiciously. 'That seems a mighty coincidence.'

'Not at all,' said Mr Gout. 'I believe it is the very

reason Mr Harding summoned me here in the first place.'

I frowned. 'But how could he have known that? You had never met before, had you?'

'No. But we had one connection: the Earl.'

'You know the Earl?' asked Mrs Jones.

'I did, many years ago. We have not seen each other for decades, but it would seem he remembers some of our interactions. He must have spoken of me to Mr Harding.'

Mrs Jones looked suspicious, but said nothing further. My own mind was a whirl of a thousand questions. So not only did Mr Gout know the Earl, as his son had intimated, but he knew him well enough that he thought it possible for the Earl to have passed on stories about him, and indeed his interaction with supernatural forces, to his staff! I didn't blame Mrs Jones for being suspicious. I knew about the curse, and I still found it hard to understand how Mr Gout could have forgotten all about his connection to the Earl until now. I smothered a sigh. Clearly, I would not get any answers now. But I would be damned if my master and I weren't going to have a serious conversation in the near future.

'So how are we going to do this?' I asked. 'What did you do last time?'

'Mr Harding was on the right path; he just got careless. He neglected to use the proper protections. We will not make the same mistake.'

'What sort of protections?' asked Mrs Jones.

'Like weapons? Would a gun work on a ghost?'

'No, more like armour,' Mr Gout explained. 'A protective circle, in fact. Drawn in salt, for preference.'

'That's it? It's as simple as that?'

'In a manner of speaking, but there is one other important element. We cannot allow the statue to actually be destroyed. If we do, it will destroy whatever is left of Thomas.'

'But isn't that sort of what we want?'

'No. If we do, we risk never finding Sally. We don't know where he's taken her, or what state she is in. We need to follow the owl back to her.'

'So we need to burn the statue, but not burn it?' I said.

'We need to burn it just enough to draw him out, then remove it from the fire before it goes too far. Some sort of chain should work, something we can wrap around that won't burn. There is one other problem, however.'

'Oh really, just one?' Mrs Jones said, looking less than confident.

'Yes. We cannot place the fire within the protective circle. If we do, it will be shielded from Thomas and he will not come.'

'So...you're saying someone will have to leave the protective circle to remove the statue from the fire once the owl arrives. That sounds...unwise,' I said.

'Quite. Our friend Mr Harding has made a good example of what would happen if we attempted that. So that is where the chain comes in. We can yank the statue out of the fire from a safe distance. If we do this right, there is no need for Thomas to even know we are here.'

'I have two questions,' I said. 'First, if the statue is such a source of weakness to this thing, then why didn't it just take it when it killed Mr Harding? Why leave it, making itself vulnerable? Second, assuming this all goes to plan, how do we make sure we can track him back to Sally?'

'To answer your first question,' said Mr Gout. 'He certainly would have taken the statue had he been able to find it.'

'But it obviously did!' Mrs Jones cut in.

'Look, you can't think of this entity like a person. It will have been drawn here, yes. But unless the statue was obvious, out in the open, which clearly it was not, being buried in the fire, it wouldn't have searched for it. It wouldn't think as clearly as that. Don't forget, it's operating mostly on instinct. We're lucky the statue didn't burn up completely, because the owl would have been powerless to stop it. Fortunately, the fire did not completely destroy it. However, to answer the second part of your question, we must achieve exactly this. We must make the statue obvious enough that the bird will take it.'

'Why?'

'Because that way we can track it. I have a handy little tracing spell that will do just the job. But we must get Thomas to take the statue.'

Mrs Jones gaped at him. 'A tracking spell? Just who are you people, really?'

'My dear woman, the nature of our work can often seem surprising, or strange to the uninitiated. But I assure you we only want what is best for all involved. You need not fear the, ahem, *stranger* aspects of the craft. We are professionals, I assure you.'

I thought of the very first time I had seen Mr Gout perform a spell, just a few months before in the attic bedroom of my granny. As I recalled, there had been more than a little chaos and he had inadvertently been covered in the contents of my granny's bed pan. Admittedly, that had been at least partly my fault, but it hardly spoke of professionalism. That day, it happened in a flash. I had jumped into the fray with barely a thought, except to save my grandmother. This was different, though, and I felt a little sick at the idea of what he was suggesting. I kept my thoughts to myself, however, all too aware that my reticence might rub off on the others if I showed it.

Mr Gout gave me a small smile and winked, as if he had read my thoughts. He then turned to address the cook. 'Come, Mrs Jones. We have much to prepare before the light fades.'

Dusk found us gathered once more in the clearing where Mr Harding had met his unfortunate end. His body had been removed and now lay under a sheet in the Hall's cellar. The Earl's son's eyes had nearly popped out of his head when he had staggered out of his study to find the body of his deceased gamekeeper being processed through his hallways. After he had stopped shouting, he had, of course, demanded to know what had happened. Which parts he believed were anyone's guess, but he now stood as part of the group as the light faded around us. He looked at the darkening sky, then around the woodland, with obvious distaste.

'Just how long is this cock-a-manny scheme going to take? I'd quite like not to be stumbling around the bloody woods at midnight,' he asked loudly, breaking the tense silence that had fallen upon our little group.

There were four of us in total. Myself, Mr Gout, Mrs Jones and the Earl's son himself. The rest of the servants had been given strict instructions not to leave the Hall till daybreak. There had been some pushback on this, but Mr Gout had promised to call for aid, should it be required. In the end it was Mrs Jones who convinced them, using sharp words I will not repeat here. Whatever befell us in the woods that night, we would find no help coming from the hall, unless we specifically asked for it.

Mr Gout shot the man a quickly buried look of annoyance, before answering his question with another. 'Do you have an important engagement to attend? A nice dinner, perhaps, as one of your staff lies somewhere in your grounds, in mortal peril?' He said it lightly enough, but his feelings were clear.

The Earl's son scowled. 'I was just asking,' he

said.

'It should take exactly as long as it needs to,' my master said enigmatically. 'Any longer than that will be due to pointless interruptions. Now, I think we have reached the opportune time. Perhaps you can make yourself useful and help me with the fire.'

The man looked about to argue, but obviously thought better of it. He silently followed Mr Gout over to where the old garden incinerator had been placed, emptied and ready for service once again. A pile of twigs and firewood had been left next to it and the two men began to build the fire.

Mrs Jones stood next to me and wrung her hands. 'This is going to work, isn't it?' she asked.

I hefted the long chain that I had curled in a reel further up onto my shoulder before answering. 'Mr Gout is very experienced at this sort of thing. Just be ready.'

She nodded and fell silent. Truthfully, I still had my own misgivings about the whole affair. My master projected his usual confident, unflappable exterior, but I could tell he was troubled. He had been ever since we'd arrived at Thicklewood Hall. There was something he wasn't telling me, and that worried me. But I had decided to focus on the job at hand, and that was rescuing poor Sally. I needed to keep my wits about me.

Soon, thin curls of purple smoke were rising from the cracking incinerator. Mr Gout stepped back, rubbing his hands together. 'Excellent,' he said. 'Clementine, my dear, I think it's time you attached the statue to that chain of yours.'

I did so, wrapping the chain tightly around the burnt lump of wood I had rescued from the incinerator just hours before. It didn't even look much like an owl anymore. I just hoped the owl – Thomas – would turn up quick enough, before the whole thing crumbled into ashes.

'Now then,' Mr Gout was saying. 'Is everybody clear about their roles before we start?' He pointed to the cook, who trembled quietly and looked pale in the dusk light.

'I'm to drop the statue in the fire. But not before everyone else is safely within the protective circle. Then I'm to hurry to the circle myself, and stay there.'

'Yes, indeed. No matter what happens, mind,' Mr Gout reminded her. 'I shall begin the circle momentarily, as it will take several minutes to prepare. My Lord, since you have insisted on accompanying us, your role, if you please?'

The Earl's son looked less than happy at being addressed so, but complied. 'I am to ensure the circle is not broken. Something that you have so far failed to explain to me how I am supposed to achieve.'

'And that shall be rectified momentarily,' Mr Gout said. 'Miss Trussel?'

I swallowed, my mouth dry. 'I am to keep a tight hold on this chain, pulling the statue clear of the flames once we have the owl in sight.'

'Quite right. But not before I have added the final component to the tracking spell. It is a simple incantation that I can achieve from the safety of the circle, so that should pose no problem.'

'Would it not be easier to do that now? Why complicate things at the crucial time?' said the Earl's son.

Mr Gout shook his head. 'It must be done at the last possible moment. It is a reliable spell, but time-sensitive. We will have but one hour to find Sally from the moment I utter the final syllable.'

'An hour!' Mrs Jones looked shocked. 'Will that be enough time? What if it takes us longer than that to follow the owl back to its lair?'

'If its lair is that far away, it will not reach us before the flames entirely consume the statue, so the point will be moot,' Mr Gout said. 'But do not worry. I am confident that the creature cannot be hidden too far away.'

'How can you be sure?' asked the Earl's son.

'Because if it were, then poor Mr Harding would most likely still be alive. No, it must be close. So we must be ready. Come, let us begin.'

I let my mind wander as I crouched on the cold, damp woodland floor. Mr Gout was slowly circling us, reading from his well-worn leather notebook, muttering incantations under his breath, and pouring a steady stream of white powder onto the ground in a wide arc. I knew once he was finished, and the plan began, I would have to remain sharp as a tack, so I could afford a little daydreaming now. It mostly seemed to be focused on food. We had somehow forgotten dinner in all the fuss, and lunch.

It seemed a long time ago we had been sitting with Mrs Jones in the kitchen with cake, and Mr Gout had eaten mine, anyway. But it made me think again of how oddly my master was behaving. He had also not eaten since then, a feat I would have believed impossible until that day. He was clearly distracted, and not just by the matter at hand. I wondered again just what the Earl's son had meant when he held me back in his study and warned me off Mr Gout. I would have to find the right moment to talk to him again. I trusted Mr Gout, but there was so much about him I did not know.

Once the circle was complete, Mr Gout handed his powder to the Earl's son, who took it reluctantly, a grimace on his face as if he were being handed something unspeakable.

'If at any point my work is disturbed, and the circle is broken, all you have to do is use this to repair it,' said Mr Gout.

'Won't the protective spell be broken, though?' I asked.

He shook his head. 'A slight break, quickly filled, should not disrupt our protection. You must be quick though,' he warned the Earl's son, who nodded sullenly.

'And what about a large break?' asked Mrs Jones nervously. 'What happens then?'

Mr Gout regarded her seriously. 'If for some reason a large amount of the circle is disturbed, then, yes, our protection will be lost. So I must impress on you all the importance of not allowing that to happen. If all goes awry, and it does, then run. Run as fast as you can and don't stop until you find shelter.'

His words seemed to do little to reassure the group, and a tense silence followed. They were undoubtedly imagining the worst, as was I.

Mr Gout offered us a reassuring smile. 'Come, friends. Do not worry. We are prepared. Do as I tell you and you will be in no danger. Let us begin.' He nodded to Mrs Jones, who visibly gulped. As she approached the blazing incinerator, Mr Gout motioned for the rest of us to enter the protective circle. The trembling cook held the owl statue, still wrapped in the chain, which snaked back across the grass, its end in my own hands. She made sure we were all safely within the protective circle, then dropped the owl and hurried back to rejoin us. Taking the chain up in my hand, I tensed, ready to pull the statue free at the right moment. Mr Gout nodded. 'Good. Now we wait.'

We waited. I suddenly became all too aware of how chilly the wood had become now that the sun was sinking. Goosebumps broke out across my arms and I shivered in my dress. I should have brought a coat. We crouched next to each other in silence. This seemed to amplify the sounds of the surrounding woods, which were alive with the evening call of birds. A fox barked somewhere in the distance, and I shivered again. I wondered how long it would take for the owl to show up. Would it come at all?

As the minutes passed, and darkness took a

proper hold of the clearing, the birdsong petered out and I feared for the state of the statue in the flames. I caught Mr Gout's eye and opened my mouth to speak, but he shook his head silently and held a finger to his lips. I remained silent, my anxiety increasing with each passing second. I could feel the tension of the others, too. Even the scowl on the Earl's son's face was tempered by fear.

And then all at once the owl was upon us. It – Thomas – exploded out of the woodland gloom and into the clearing with a mad flutter of wings and a screech that went through me like a hook in my sternum. My hands tensed on the chain in my grasp, even before Mr Gout, eyes wide, gave me the signal I'd been waiting for. I yanked on the chain with all my might and was rewarded with a loud clanging sound and a spray of orange sparks as the incinerator toppled over. The owl circled the clearing at speed, its fierce eyes fixed on the falling can and the flaming wood that spilled out across the grass. It screeched again, and it was a sound of such anger and pain my breath caught in my throat.

I knew immediately something had gone wrong. We had planned so fastidiously, and yet the plan was undone by the simplest part. When I pulled the chain, it had overturned the incinerator, but in the process the statue had come loose and was now lying in a heap of burning wood. I had no way to move it further from where I crouched and even at this distance, I could see the thing was becoming dangerously close to being completely consumed.

THE WHITE OWL OF THICKLEWOOD HALL

The owl spiralled round and round the clearing, calling angrily, yet not daring to approach the fire.

'We've got a problem,' I said.

'Don't leave the circle!' Mr Gout reminded me, throwing his arm back as if to stop me whilst staring at the circling bird.

'But what do we do? At this rate, it will be destroyed and then we'll have no way of finding Sally!'

I watched the large man as he looked out at the scene, his eyes calculating. 'I'll have to make a dash for it,' he said, getting to his feet.

'NO!' I hissed, following suit. 'We can't take that risk. You're the only one who can complete the tracking spell. I'll do it!'

Without waiting for approval, I stepped out of the circle.

The effect was immediate. The white owl's huge, milky eyes snapped to me and it gave its loudest screech yet, turning in mid-air and swooping down on me with frightening speed. Ignoring the cries of my master from behind, I wasted no time. Sprinting for the burning pile, I ducked and rolled across the grass to avoid the owl's outstretched talons. I felt them catch on my hair as it sailed over my head. Regaining my feet, I continued my momentum and reached the fire, kicking out a desperate foot that connected with the burning statue and sent it bouncing off across the grass. I followed, stamping on it tentatively, rolling it in the grass to extinguish the burning. A cry from behind me made me turn and see that the owl was bearing down on me again. I threw myself to one side, but not quickly enough, a single talon raking my cheek. I cried out in pain as I hit the ground and the owl screamed as if in answer.

'Get back to the circle!' I heard Mr Gout yell.

Struggling to my feet, I intended to comply, but the owl had other plans. It had swooped round again for another attack, but this time, instead of flying at me, wings out, talons raised, it landed, mere feet away.

Then it began to change.

First it seemed to swell, doubling in size, then becoming three feet tall, four, five, until suddenly I was facing a beast taller than myself and considerably larger. Its features, too, were shifting, becoming more human. It was a winged man that bore down on me now, its face still avian, still filled by its white eyes and vicious beak. I stumbled backwards blindly, shying away from the sheer aura of menace emanating from the creature.

It launched itself at me and I screamed, falling down again, the weight of the owl, Thomas, crushing down on top of me. The smell of earth and decay enveloped me until I nearly choked on the stench.

I think he would have killed me right there. Gutted me with those horrifying winged arms, which ended in hands that themselves ended more in talons than fingers. I saw him ready to make the blow, hatred pouring from his milky white eyes. Powerless, I screwed my own shut and braced against the coming pain.

But it never arrived.

Instead, I heard the thud of running feet, then a roar of rage, and suddenly something hit us and we were both sprawling across the grass. When the world stopped spinning, my eyes flew open. The creature and Mr Gout were struggling together on the ground a few feet from where I lay. For a moment it seemed my master had the upper hand, but even as I watched, Thomas kicked out with taloned feet and Mr Gout fell back with a cry. His shirt was ripped and bloody, great crimson patches spreading across his chest within seconds. Thomas was back on his feet and advancing.

'NO!' I screamed, my hand searching in the grass for any kind of weapon I could use to defend my master. It found a rock, and I threw it with all my might, hitting the owl-man between his hunched shoulders.

It bounced off its feathers like it had hit a mattress, but it was enough to make the creature pause and turn again in my direction. That was all the time Mr Gout needed to scrabble to his feet.

'RUN!' he shouted at me, but his face was such a mask of terror I was momentarily rooted to the spot. This was my master, Theophilius Gout, truly and utterly afraid. I felt his fear wash over me like a wave, mixing and mingling with my own until it was all I could do to stop myself from screwing shut my eyes again and lying, trembling, on the floor.

This was not how it was supposed to go.
Theophilius Gout was not meant to be afraid.

PART SIX

For a moment, nobody moved. Then, with another guttural cry of rage, Mr Gout threw himself again at the creature.

'Get back in the circle!' he grunted at me again as he grappled with Thomas. The revenant seemed to be taken aback by the ferocity of his opponent's attack, but I knew it would not be long before he recovered. When that happened, I didn't like my master's chances.

I had to think.

There had to be something.

Anything!

Of course! The statue!

I had all but forgotten the thing in the struggle, but it was still lying in the grass where I had dropped it. I forced my legs into action and ran over, scooping it up, then turning and waving it over my head like a crazy person.

'Hey!' I yelled. 'Thomas! Thomas Harding! I have your statue! I have Sally's statue!'

I thought the creature was ignoring me, intent on his fight with Mr Gout, but at the mention of his erstwhile fiancée's name, his beaked face locked onto me with the disturbing intensity of a bird of prey. He screamed, a sound as much human as bird, then shoved Mr Gout aside, never taking those horrid white eyes off me, his head perfectly still, perfectly trained on me as he moved.

'NO!' Mr Gout cried out as he fell. 'Clementine, don't! Get back to the circle!'

But that was exactly my plan. Now I had Thomas's attention, I heaved the statue with all my might in an overarm throw as far from me, Mr Gout and the others in the protective circle as I could manage. Then I ran.

I expected Thomas to launch himself after the thing. It was what he wanted, after all, and indeed his head followed the statue as it arced through the air. But I had underestimated his speed. With a frighteningly rapid lunge forward, he met the spinning object mid-air and snapped at it with his wicked beak, catching it with ease.

I realised too late what was going to happen next.

With a surge of movement, he extended his clawed feet out in front of him and used his forward momentum to bear down on me. A white-hot pain seared across my shoulders as his claws dug in, and I screamed. Then, with a mighty beat of his outstretched wings, Thomas rose into the air. The pain in my shoulders increased tenfold, and I felt my feet leave the ground. Through tear-stained eyes I saw the woodland floor drop away as, with more beats of his powerful wings, the revenant took us higher and higher into the canopy of trees. Bare branches scraped at me as we rose and I was aware of Mr Gout bellowing below me, but I couldn't make out the words.

Then something hit my head, there was an explosion of stars in front of my eyes, and it all went black.

I awoke with a start, pain throbbing behind my eyes, so extreme I retched blindly, bringing up nothing.

'Oh thank god, you're alive!'

In my confusion, I did not recognise the voice. My mind reeled.

Where was I? What had happened?

The memories came back in a confusing flood. So did the pain in my shoulders. I whimpered.

'Shhh…it's okay. You're okay,' said the voice. But whoever it was sounded scared.

I tried to open my eyes.

I was in…what was I in? It looked and felt like some sort of log pile. No, not logs exactly. Branches. And there were feathers, and…

My eyes flew fully open as I realised what it was with a cold, leaden dread in my stomach.

I was in a nest.

Something touched my arm, and I flinched back instinctively.

'It's alright, it's me. It's Sally, miss.'

Through my rising panic, I focused on the girl knelt over me. It was indeed the maid, Sally. She was dirty and dishevelled, the scratches down her face still livid and red, but she seemed otherwise unharmed. I pushed myself up onto my elbows and then allowed her to help me into a sitting position. Then I looked around. We really were in a giant nest. A mass of branches, feathers and…other stuff I decided not to investigate too closely. The structure was built wedged in between the trunks of three large trees, maybe fifty feet above the ground. I looked over the edge and my head swam.

'Easy,' Sally said, steadying me as another wave of nausea washed over me.

I closed my eyes again until it passed.

'Where…?' I managed.

'It's alright. He's not here. But he won't be far.'

'How long was I out?'

Sally shrugged. 'Maybe twenty minutes? It's hard to tell out here.'

'And you're alright?' I asked.

Sally gave a small smile. 'Apart from being held captive by the…I don't know what of my dead fiancé? Yes, I'm fine.'

This grabbed my full attention. 'You know the owl is Thomas?'

The maid looked surprised in turn. '*You* know the owl is Thomas?'

'We figured it out, yes. Especially after we found…' I paused, but Sally finished the sentence for me.

'Mr Harding, dead?'

I nodded. 'Did he...did he hurt you?'

Sally shook her head. 'He didn't really get a chance.'

'What *happened*?' I asked. 'We eventually figured out he hadn't taken you to the Hall after the owl...after Thomas attacked you–'

'Thomas never attacked me!' Sally cut in, a spark of anger in her eyes. 'He was trying to attack his brother, not me.'

I paused and looked at her set expression. 'Right,' I said. 'Actually, that makes more sense. Well, eventually Mrs Jones filled us in about what happened to Thomas, how you were engaged to him, how he fell out with his brother before he died. We guessed some of the rest, but...' I let the question hang in the air.

Sally looked uncomfortable. 'Is now really the time to get into all that?'

She had a point, but...

I tried to marshal my thoughts.

'It's alright,' I said. 'Help is on the way.' If I was here, I reasoned, then the statue must be too. Indeed, a quick glance around confirmed this, as I spotted it bedded into the centre of the nest. I just had to hope Mr Gout had managed to complete the tracking spell in all the chaos. I shifted my weight and my shoulders gave another deep throb of pain, making me groan.

'You're hurt,' Sally said, her expression pained.

'I'm sorry. When he bought you here, I thought for a moment…well, it doesn't matter what I thought.'

Something about the way she said it made me pause. Why would *she* be sorry for what the owl had done? Then understanding hit me in a flash.

'You've known the whole time, haven't you? That the owl was Thomas, I mean. You've known since before it attacked you.'

Sally scowled. '*I* was never attacked! Thomas would never…'

I raised my eyebrows, and she touched the wounds on her face self-consciously.

'I told you, that was an accident,' she said. "Thomas didn't mean to hurt me.'

So she *had* known. But something still did not make sense.

I clutched my banging head and tried to think.

'It's clear that Mr Harding – Terence, I mean, not Thomas…lured us all there that night. He *wanted* you attacked, or at least for it to look like that. He needed the excuse to take you away. But then why summon Mr Gout? He could have taken you any time.' I tried to concentrate, my mind sluggish. 'The cart!' I said at length. 'He told us to come straight to his cottage. He knew we'd have a cart, travelling so far. For his escape, he needed that. But it seems a bit convoluted. Surely there were easier ways…'

The facts danced through my muddled mind, slipping out of focus every time I tried to shine a light on them.

'It wasn't just the cart. That was a bonus,' I continued. 'He needed my master to deal with the owl.'

'His name is Thomas!' Sally said, her voice sharp.

'Yes, yes. Thomas. Mr Harding knew the owl was Thomas the whole time too. He summoned my master, hoping he would kill it...*him*.' I tutted in annoyance. 'No, that can't be right! He already knew how to destroy Thomas. He knew to burn the owl statue.'

'The statue?' Sally's eyes drifted to the charred lump, still just distinguishable as the owl it had once been. 'What has that got to do with anything?'

'It is the object Thomas is tethered to,' I explained impatiently, still racking my brain for the answers. 'So if he knew how to kill his brother, once and for all, then why wait? Why summon an expert in the paranormal?'

'*That's* what your master is?' Sally said, her mouth dropping open.

I ignored the question, looking at her instead. 'I'm missing something,' I said. 'And I think you know what it is?'

Sally sighed, then to my surprise, gave a nervous little laugh. 'Well, I suppose none of it matters anymore, does it? I may as well tell you.'

But still she was silent for a moment before she spoke again. When she did, her voice was weary. 'Terence...the man you know as Mr Harding, well, he was always jealous of my relationship with Thomas.

I was naive, perhaps, but I always thought that he disliked me because I was taking Thomas away from him. They'd always been close and, well, Terence didn't really have anyone else. Thomas was always the personable one. I never realised that Terence had…other desires. Looking back, I think Thomas must have hidden a lot from me about his brother.'

'So Mr Harding…sorry, *Terence*, he made a pass at you? That's why he fell out with his brother?' I asked, massaging my aching skull with tentative fingers.

Sally nodded. 'In a nutshell. It happened one night when I took Terence his supper. I was so shocked I ran. I think that hurt him more than anything else. He hadn't been violent… it was nothing like that. He just…well, he surprised me. I genuinely had no idea he felt that way about me. Of course, the first thing I did was tell Thomas.'

Sally fell silent for a moment, staring at the bed of branches beneath her knees. 'Things were never the same after that. Thomas never told me what was said between them when he confronted Terence. But they spoke little after.'

'That can't have been easy,' I said, shivering and wrapping my arms around myself. It was cold up in the nest and I lamented not bringing a coat once again. 'When you all worked together at the Hall, I mean.'

Sally shrugged. 'It's a big estate. Mostly I think Terence was embarrassed. He kept his distance. I only really saw him when I dropped off his supper.'

'You still did that?' I asked, shocked.

Sally gave another shrug. 'It was part of my job, miss. To not do it would mean explaining to Mrs Jones and Mr Perkins why. We, Thomas and I, didn't want that for Terence.'

I frowned. 'You seem awfully forgiving.'

'It was one mistake,' Sally said. 'At first…'

'It happened again?'

'No. No, he never touched me again…until last night. He just got angry. It changed him. Do you know what I mean? That rage. It was in him all the time. He'd always been a difficult person to get to know. That was just his way. But now he was downright hostile. Anyway, about two months later I took him his supper one night, and he was especially…'

Here Sally paused again, and gave a little sniff, then shook herself. 'I don't need to repeat the things he said to me. It's not important, not really. The words hurt at the time, but they were just words. I tried to tell Thomas that…'

'But he went to confront his brother again?' I guessed.

'That's right.' The maid's face seemed to pale at the thought, her eyes growing distant. 'I will regret letting him go that night till the day I die,' she said, her voice choked.

'That was the night he was killed?' I asked in a soft voice.

She nodded, her eyes wet.

We were both silent for a while after that. I

knew very well that the owl could return at any moment, and equally aware that there was nothing I could do about it from our current position. I eyed the trees supporting the nest, wondering if we might somehow climb to safety. But it looked fairly hopeless. The ground was a long way away, and my stomach churned and head swam just looking over the edge. Anyway, escape would hinge on my companion actually *wanting* to, and I was starting to suspect that Sally had no intention of leaving.

'Did you not tell anyone about what had happened? I mean, when Thomas turned up dead, surely your suspicions must have fallen on his brother?' I said.

She scowled at me. 'Of course they did! I am not some air-headed fool, girl! I guessed what must have happened, even if I could scarcely believe it of Terence. I took my concerns to the master straight away, only...'

I closed my eyes, knowing what must have happened. I could practically see the disbelieving expression the Earl's son's face. 'He didn't take you seriously?'

Sally gave a bitter laugh. 'There was no evidence, he said.'

'And the police?'

'Wouldn't take the word of some maid over the son of an Earl,' Sally said, with feeling.

I tried to take this all in. 'So why were you still bringing Mr Harding his supper? You had good reason to believe the man had murdered his own brother!'

At my words Sally deflated, the anger leaving her all at once, to be replaced by weary resignation.

'What should I have done instead? Refused? Continued to shout his guilt from the rooftops until I was sacked and thrown out on the streets? You're young, but you're not *that* young. This world is not kind to a woman with no family and no position. Besides, after a while, even I began to wonder if I wasn't wrong about Terence. He'd always been many things, but not violent, not as far as I knew.'

'So you stayed,' I said.

'I stayed...and I waited. For what, I didn't know. But then a miracle happened. Then my Thomas came back to me.'

I eyed the darkness nervously as she said this, expecting to see the ghostly form of the owl-man sweeping out of the gloom. But all was still and quiet. I sorely hoped Mr Gout and the others were on the way.

'How did you know he was the owl?' I asked.

Sally smiled, but sadly. 'It is hard to explain. Have you ever known when a loved one has entered a room, even before you've seen them? Well, it was a bit like that. The first time I saw him, I just...knew.'

'None of this explains what Mr Harding... Terence...was up to!' I said in frustration. 'He knew just what the owl was, and he knew enough to burn the statue.'

'That's the bit I don't understand,' Sally said. 'I guessed he recognised his brother, just like I did. But the statue. How did he figure that out?'

'That's…complicated,' I said.

Sally threw her arms out, indicating the surrounding canopy. 'I'm not going anywhere.'

I sighed. 'Look, I don't totally understand it myself. But, my master has come across a revenant once before, or so he tells me. And it also turns out he knew the Earl in his youth.'

'*Our* Earl?' Sally said, eyebrows rising.

'Yes, it would seem so. Anyway, Mr Gout thinks that the Earl must have mentioned his dealings with Mr Gout to Mr Harding, including something about this previous revenant.'

Sally looked sceptical. 'If he did, it must have been a long time ago. The Earl hasn't been to Thicklewood in years.'

'Well, Mrs Jones did say the brothers practically grew up on the estate,' I pointed out.

'True. But even so, it all seems very…' she trailed off.

I could not blame her for being dubious. I scarcely understood the connection myself.

'Well, whatever the case may be, that's the only explanation we have for how he knew what to do with the statue. Also how he knew to write to Mr Gout. But not *why*!'

'That I think I do know,' Sally admitted, although she seemed reluctant.

I stared at her expectantly and she fidgeted, but spoke. 'I'm afraid Terence was planning to frame you for my murder.'

'*What?*'

Sally shrugged, looking miserable. 'He as much as told me in the woods last night.'

'But that…that is *horrible!*' I said. 'I thought he was trying to kidnap you, not…'

'It was hard to tell precisely what he had in mind,' Sally said in a heavy voice. 'He wasn't making much sense. To be honest, I think his brother's return finally pushed him over the edge. His mind was gone. He wasn't the man I used to know, not anymore.' She gave another sigh and a shiver. 'But I think he wanted me dead. It might have been because he hated me. Or it might have been because I was a constant reminder of what he'd done. It hardly matters now. What I do know is that he had no intention of taking me any further than where we stopped with your wagon in the woods. It was like… like he was setting the scene.'

I shook my head. 'But if he really wanted you dead, why go to all that trouble?'

'Think about it,' Sally said. 'With his brother… well, despite everything, I truly believe he never set out to kill Thomas. I think it was an accident. A terrible crime committed in the heat of the moment. But with me, I think he planned this for a long time. He got away with the murder of his brother, but if I suddenly turned up dead too, then even the master would have to start asking questions.'

'So he needed someone to blame it on,' I said. 'And who better than a stranger who claims to deal with the supernatural? And we played right into his hands!'

'It would have looked like some kind of, I don't know, *exorcism* gone wrong?' Sally said. 'Me, dead in the woods, the very night a stranger turns up on the estate to kill the demon owl Terence had been warning people about for weeks. If it hadn't been for Thomas turning up when Terence tried to burn the statue…'

'He'd have got away with it,' I said, horrified.

Sally nodded. 'And I would be dead. So no, Thomas never attacked me. He saved me.'

'Is that why you haven't tried to escape?' I asked.

Sally gave a humourless smirk. 'You mean besides being stuck fifty feet up a tree? Yes. Look, I'm not stupid. I know Thomas is…not quite himself. I might not be some fancy paranormal investigator, but I can tell that much. But he's still my Thomas, and while even a tiny scrap of the man I love is still in this world, then no, I'll not leave him. Not for you or your Mr Gout. Not for anybody.'

'He's dangerous, Sally,' I said. 'Surely you see that? Mr Gout says he will only become more unstable.'

What Sally might have said to that I never found out. Because it was at that moment her dead fiancé returned.

I say he returned, but in truth, it soon became clear he had never left. Our first warning was the sounds of something moving about in the woods below. The crack of dry branches, then voices, faint but definitely heading our way. My heart leapt, and I hurriedly crawled to the edge of the nest, looking down towards the dark ground. I couldn't see anyone yet, but who else could it be but Mr Gout and the rescue party? A grin spread across my face as I drew breath, filling my lungs in order to shout out to them. But a much closer sound caused the air to catch in my throat. Something large was shifting about in the branches above; the scraping of wood and the hard, hollow crack of branch hitting branch that sounded like bones knocking together.

I looked up, already knowing what I would see.

The owl-man was clawing his way around the thick trunk of a tree just a few feet away. He had clearly been hanging there, just out of sight the entire time. His monstrous head turned in our direction. Then he dropped, plummeting towards the woodland floor in perfect silence, before extending his huge wings and pulling up, soaring into the night in the direction of the voices.

For a second my fear of the thing overcame me, and all that issued from my mouth was a half-strangled hiss. But I had to warn them. If I didn't, and the owl-man dropped right out of the sky on to their heads…

'Look out!'

I cried the words with all my might, but the dark forest seemed to eat the sound. Then from somewhere in the distance came the sound of people shouting, though still I could see nothing in the blackness below.

I swore furiously and tried to get to my feet. Sally exclaimed in surprise, a reaction that struck me as faintly ridiculous, given the circumstances.

'Come on!' I snapped, attempting to climb over the ridge of the nest where it met one of the three trees.

'What are you doing?' she hissed in response.

'We have to help them!' I managed to get to the tree, then slowly, on wobbling legs, my back against the rough bark of the trunk, stood.

'Are you crazy? We'll fall to our deaths!'

I ignored her. There was a branch just a couple of feet below me to the right. If I got my positioning right, I felt sure I could drop down onto it.

'Stop!' Sally cried. 'For goodness' sake, girl, are you mad?'

'Stay here if you want,' I said. 'But I'm going to help.'

And I jumped.

The branch hit me in the stomach with a blow that felt like it might split me in two. It forced the breath from my lungs in a single whoosh, but I clamped my arms and legs around the wooden limb as if my life depended on it. It very probably did.

'Are you alright?' Sally's pale face appeared over the edge of the nest.

'Splendid,' I muttered.

'This is insanity! What will you even do if you get down without breaking your neck?'

'I'm…going…to help…Mr Gout…' I said, my

words punctuated as I carefully lowered myself on the branch immediately below my new position.

'Help him do what, exactly?' came the worried voice from above. 'Not…not hurt Thomas?'

My feet hit wood, and I balanced for a moment, hands resting on the branch above, and looked up at her. 'Look, if you're concerned, you'd better come with me, hadn't you?'

Then I continued my treacherous descent. Sally didn't call down again, but not long after I heard the scrape of her boots from above and a few muttered words.

'Insanity…*insanity*.'

I strained my ears to pick out what was happening out of sight below. There were continued shouts of alarm and possibly the sounds of a fight. I cursed again and urged my aching limbs to go faster. Of course, Sally had a point, not that I was going to admit that to her. Just exactly what *did* I think I could do to help stop Thomas? I'd barely escaped our last fight with my life. But I had to do something. Anything I could. Even if I was just a distraction to allow Mr Gout to do…whatever it was he intended to do to neutralise the revenant.

It took several torturous minutes, but at long last, the woodland floor below became more distinct. It must have been barely fifteen feet away now. I was considering my next move when there came a loud *crack* from above and Sally screamed. I looked up, just in time to get a face full of boot as the maid came crashing down on top of me. My hands were wrenched from their grip and we were falling, entwined together, branches and twigs snatching at our clothes as we fell, snapping beneath us as we carved our way towards the ground.

We landed with an almighty thump and my neck jarred badly, my teeth rattling in my head. I lay for a moment, stunned, but still alive.

'Are you alright?' I asked, stars in my eyes.

A low groan was my only response, but it meant the maid wasn't dead.

I carefully extracted my limbs from Sally's and staggered to my feet, looking about. The sounds of a fight were clearer now, and I was sure I could make out Mr Gout's booming voice. Sally rolled over with another groan, then her face winced.

'Are you hurt?' I asked.

She shook her head. 'I'll be fine. It's just my ankle.'

I helped her to her feet, and she hopped on one leg, wincing again, sucking in air through clenched teeth. 'I think it's sprained,' she explained and put the other foot down slowly, testing it out.

'Can you walk?' I looked anxiously towards the sound of the fight.

'I think so,' Sally said. 'But not run. Go. I'll follow. Don't let them hurt my Thomas!' She squeezed my arm painfully, and I had to nod before she'd let me go. Then I was away, stumbling in the direction I thought the others must be, wondering if I had just lied to the woman. I didn't know, if it came to it, if there was any way I could help Thomas. But I shoved those thoughts to the back of my mind. I had to reach them first.

I could make out a faint white glow ahead. That could only be one thing. I spurred my aching, battered body to greater efforts. Then, seemingly all at once, I was upon them.

I raced through a loose cluster of trees and emerged into a clearing that was full of chaos. The first thing my eyes were drawn to was the startlingly white figure of Thomas, who, even as I watched, came screeching out of the air at the other figures below. I saw Mrs Jones fall onto her back with a shriek. The Earl's son dived to one side, landing in a thick patch of scrub. The call for help had obviously been sent to the Hall after all, because two servants whose names I did not know were hiding behind trees. This left just one man in the revenant's path. Mr Gout stood firm, one hand outstretched towards the creature, the other grasping his open notebook. He was muttering an incantation under his breath.

I registered all this in a single moment, and in the next was hurling myself into the clearing, into the path of the swooping owl-man. I hit Thomas in the side, getting a face full of feathers. He was forced away from hitting my master and landed awkwardly a few feet away, his clawed feet ploughing a furrow in the leaf mould. Mr Gout looked up at me in surprise. His hand had begun to glow with a bright white light to rival the revenant's own.

'Stay back!' he barked, then swung his outstretched arm round to where Thomas crouched, already preparing to launch himself back into the sky. With a cry in a language I did not understand, Mr Gout launched the ball of glowing light from his fingertips at Thomas as he sprang. It hit the owl-man in the chest and he screeched in anger, forced again to alter his path and instead swoop up into the sky and land in a tree at the edge of the clearing. Was it my imagination, or was he smaller now than he had been? It was as if the light, whatever it was, that Mr Gout hit him with had sucked out some of his power.

'I need time!' Mr Gout shouted without looking at me. 'One more good hit should do it! Keep him busy, but *keep clear*!' And he immediately launched into another muttered incantation.

All very well for you to say, I thought, stumbling into the centre of the clearing, looking around wildly for something, anything that might be of use. I spotted a small pile of rocks against a nearby tree and dove for them. I snatched one up, about the size of my palm, and in one fluid motion rolled to face Thomas and threw.

It missed him by a good twelve feet.

The revenant was clawing at the tree, getting ready for another dive. Mr Gout was still muttering, his hand beginning to glow once more. But it was a weak light still. I looked around at the others. Mrs Jones was still flat on her back, clearly petrified. All I could see of the Earl's son were his feet, sticking out of a bush. Of the other servants, there now seemed no sign. I suspected they had fled. No one seemed about to do something clever.

So I did something stupid.

'He wanted to kill her, you know!' I yelled, getting to my feet. 'Your Sally!'

Thomas's head turned to lock on to me.

'He was going to kill her and leave her body in the woods. Just like he did to you!'

Thomas gave an animalistic screech that froze the blood in my veins. I heard Mr Gout mutter faster.

'Do you want that?' I cried, my mind racing to think of what to say next. 'For Sally to go through what you did? All that pain. That suffering?'

My words were clearly upsetting the owl-man. He screeched again, shifting his weight, his talons tearing at the bark beneath them as if it were paper. I dared to take my eyes off him and glance at Mr Gout, whose hand was glowing brighter.

Just a few more seconds.

'That's right!' I yelled. 'All your sulking about and it wouldn't have done a thing! He was going to kill her, and there was nothing, *nothing,* you could do about it!'

Of course, that was a lie. He had done something very effective about it. A fact I was painfully aware of at that second, as the horrifying creature prepared to launch itself at me. But I had to keep him busy. I had to hope his confused mind wouldn't figure out I was goading him with a threat he had already neutralised.

But at that moment Mr Gout's hand shone out like a beacon, and the revenant's attention snapped back to him in an instant.

'What about me?' I screamed. 'Would you let *me* kill her? Kill your Sally! Or would you stop me? *How are you going to stop me?*'

That was all Thomas could take. With an enraged noise, half man, half bird, he launched himself from the tree in my direction. He dropped through the air like a dart, hurtling towards me, the space between us disappearing frighteningly fast. In the corner of my eye I saw Mr Gout swing his arm to follow the creature's path, his notebook falling from the other as he did so. He yelled the same unintelligible word as he had before, and the ball of light exploded from his hand in my direction. I threw myself to the ground and covered my head with my hands. I felt the air above me sizzle, felt heat on my back, and blinding light exploded, searing the trees I could see from my position on the ground into skinny, wavering silhouettes.

Then the light vanished.

All was quiet and still.

Carefully, I rolled over.

Cowed and shrunken, Thomas was simply an owl once more; albeit one of the most ghostly white. It blinked its marble-like eyes mournfully and bowed its head. Mr Gout lowered his hands. His face showed no pleasure in his victory. In fact, I'd swear that I saw a single tear roll down his mud-stained cheek, before he turned away to retrieve his notebook from the ground. When he straightened up again, his face was set. He walked towards the owl, who did not move a feather at his approach.

'I am sorry for all that was done to you, my friend,' he spoke, his voice low and gentle. 'No man deserves what has befallen you. Let me put an end to it, once and for all. But know that you go in friendship. No man living can know where you go to next, but I hope you find peace there.'

The owl raised its head, staring directly into the eyes of my master for what seemed like an age. What passed between them in those seconds I cannot say, but Mr Gout nodded once, raised the notebook in one hand and reached out towards the bird with the other. He opened his mouth to speak the final incantation that would release Thomas from this plane, but a cry of distress cut him short.

Sally hurried forward, stumbling on her injured ankle, tears flowing freely down her face. She threw herself to the ground where Thomas stood, sheltering the owl with her trembling body. 'No!' she wailed. 'Please, sir, do not do it! Do not send my Thomas where I cannot follow!'

She reached for the owl and I instinctively started forward, but halted when it turned towards her and allowed itself to be scooped into her arms. Sally hugged the bird to her chest.

Mr Gout hesitated, but he did not drop his arm, a crease appearing across his forehead.

'I know that this is hard,' he said. 'But my dear girl, surely you see that the best thing for–'

'Do not presume to tell me what is best for my Thomas!' the girl cried, her face savage. She stared hard at Mr Gout for several seconds, then her face softened, but a steely glint remained in her pale eyes. 'Forgive me, sir. I mean no disrespect, and I thank you heartily for everything you have already done for me and for my Thomas. But please, sir, please leave him to me from here on.'

Mr Gout shook his head. 'I know the pain you are feeling,' he said. 'I know it better, perhaps, than you yet know it yourself. But Thomas cannot stay in this realm. He does not belong here. He *must* move on.'

'Says who?' the girl said, sticking out her chin and pulling the owl closer to her chest. It let her, burrowing into her as if it would climb inside if it could. 'You say you know this pain, but you are not me, sir. You are not Thomas. How can you know what is right for us?'

'He is dead, Sally. He will not return,' Mr Gout said, his face crumpling with a grief that seemed all his own.

'I know that!' the girl snapped. 'I am young in years, but that does not make me blind. The Thomas I knew, the man, may well be gone. But in this creature, a part of him at least remains. You admit yourself that no one truly knows what happens to us after we move on from this realm, yet you would freely send what remains of my love onward, not knowing to what fate you send him. I beg you to leave him to me. I will look after him. I will care for him. I will love him.'

Mr Gout's arm wavered, then fell to his side.

He stared at the girl. I felt sure that he would once again refuse her request, but to my surprise he said, 'You would do this? You would give up the chance for a normal life? For you will not have one if you choose this path.'

'I would give up anything for my Thomas,' the girl said, and she kissed the owl's head, making it coo softly, the most gentle sound I had heard the poor creature make since our wagon had rolled into the Thicklewood estate.

Mr Gout regarded the unlikely couple once more. I could see the indecision on his face. I felt sure he was battling with himself. Eventually, he spoke again. 'Very well. Perhaps you are right, my dear. Perhaps it is not fair for me to superimpose my experience onto yours. Maybe…maybe this time there is another way. But you will need training…' He trailed off, raising an eyebrow in a silent question.

'If you are willing to teach me, sir, I will be the most attentive student you ever met,' Sally said, hope alive in her face.

Mr Gout nodded slowly. 'Very well. I will teach you what I know of such matters. But that may not be enough. I cannot correctly predict what may occur in the future. This is a hard road you have chosen.'

Then the maid smiled at him. 'For us, sir,' she said, hugging the owl yet closer to her still. 'It is the only road.'

PART SEVEN

There was little left to say after that. We left the Thicklewood Estate later that morning. Neither Mr Gout nor I felt much compulsion to stay, and I think the inhabitants of that lonely house were just as glad to see us go. Mr Gout had spent some time with Sally, going over the basics of what she would need to know to keep the white owl safe. She would need further instruction, and they agreed on a future date to meet. The cook, Mrs Jones, thanked us both profusely for everything we had done, but pulled me aside whilst Mr Gout was readying our horse for the return journey to Abermwyl. She looked grim.

'I fear for your safety,' she said bluntly. 'This life you have been brought into...this business of your master's. It is no place for a young lady. I urge you to think twice about whatever arrangement you have made. I believe Mr Gout to be a good man. But he is still just a man. The forces he deals with...I would not like to see your life cut short because you bet on him to keep you safe.'

I promised to consider her words, and we parted with a hug, the old woman squeezing me tight. She watched me go with an expression that I felt sure said she expected bad things in my future. It unsettled me.

Our parting with the Earl's son was even worse.

He scowled at Mr Gout, but shook his hand roughly.

'I don't pretend to understand everything that has happened,' he said. 'And frankly I have no desire to learn anything more about it. But it seems we have you to thank for bringing it to a conclusion. That being said...' and here he paused for a moment, his scowl deepening. 'I think it would be best if you were not to return to Thicklewood Hall. I know trouble when I smell it, and you, sir, stink.'

Mr Gout said nothing. He simply touched a hand to his forelock, turned and walked away. I made to follow.

'Just a moment, young lady.'

I turned back. 'If you're about to warn me away from Mr Gout, I don't need to hear it.' I said, perhaps a little more harshly than was wise, given I was speaking to the nobility. But if the man took offence, his face didn't show it.

'Perhaps you have no need of my warnings,' he said. 'I'm sure it means nothing to me either way. But death follows that man. I remember my father telling me that much. And there is something else you should know. As to what it means…that I cannot tell you and have no interest in finding out.' He paused to glower at the disappearing back of my master, then continued. 'My father attended Oxford with that man. In the same year.'

I looked at him questioningly. 'What's your point?'

He grunted in frustration. 'Silly girl! Do you not see? I mean to say that they were contemporaries. Classmates. *They were the same age*. My father is now eighty-nine. How old does your master look to you? Fifty? Sixty perhaps?'

And with that, he turned his back on me and walked away.

So our little wagon trundled away from Thicklewood Hall in just as much a pall of gloom as it had arrived. Mr Gout was distracted, deep in thoughts of his own that I did not wish to disturb. My own thoughts went round in circles, but kept coming to rest on the image of Sally, clinging on to the white owl as if her heart might break if she released it. I hoped she could find the peace she craved with what remained of the man she loved. But I confess I was not hopeful. And what of me? What of the life I had chosen? Had I thought through what it would mean for me, long term, to be trained up in a business as…*unusual* as my master's, a man I was really beginning to realise I still knew very little about? I longed to know the full story of Mr Gout's previous experience with a revenant, but even then I was hesitant to ask. I sensed it was a private wound, one I had no right to rip open any wider than the last two days had already done. But the Earl's son's last words to me echoed in my head. In the end, despite my reservation, I could stand it no longer. I broke the silence with a question.

'Who died, Mr Gout?'

Silence was my only reply. I dared not turn my head to look at him.

Then I heard him give a deep sigh, and he started talking.

'When I was a much younger man, younger indeed than you are now, my dear, I lost a brother. I say lost, but of course I do not mean that. He was not misplaced. Carelessly put aside. It would be closer to the truth to say that he was stolen from me. But of course we English rarely speak so plainly, do we? Perhaps now is the time for plainness, Miss Trussel. We have known each other for some months now, and I'm sure questions have arisen in your mind as to the exact nature of the man you have tethered your livelihood to. This is only natural, of course, and whilst I cannot pretend to be able to answer every query you might have about my life – indeed I have many of my own that I lack the ability to answer – let me try to explain this little part of it.'

He paused momentarily, and I uttered a hasty response, bought on more by embarrassment at his earnestness than by any genuine sincerity. 'Oh…you certainly do not have to tell me anything that makes you uncomfortable, sir.'

I'm not even sure he heard me. He did not turn to look in my direction, instead staring straight ahead, although I do not think it was the road before us he was seeing. 'Magic came into my life, much like it did yours. I was not expecting it. I was not ready for it. Unfortunately for my family, I had not yet earned the considerable knowledge of such things that I now possess. My brother was murdered. I could tell you he was a good man, that he did not deserve such an end, but there would be others in this world who might disagree. He chose a dark path. Did dark deeds. Deeds that cannot be undone and cannot be forgiven. But for all that, he was still my brother. The manner of his death is not particularly exciting, and if it is all the same to you, I shall not mention it further. It is enough to say that the life he led did what it was always inevitably going to do, and caught up with him. That is not important. It is what happened next that concerns us. It is what happened next that destroyed what remained of my family. For he returned, much like Thomas Harding did. Knowing so little of such matters as I did back then, it was some time before I realised the truth about the creature terrorising the village I called home.'

He lapsed into silence once more and after almost an entire minute had elapsed, I dared to let go of the question that had been burning on my lips. 'What…what did he return as?'

My master turned to face me for the first time since he had started speaking, and I was shocked to see an expression that I had never seen there before. His round face held a hurt far too deep to ever be healed. His eyes, the same eyes I was so used to seeing twinkle at me with mischievous glee, looked haunted. It was like looking through into a deeper layer of a man I thought I had grown to understand, and realising that all I knew of him was what he had let me see.

'He came back as a cat,' Mr Gout said. 'It suited him, in all honesty. He, of course, never reached my age, but even as a young man, he always had a more feline build. People have described me in many ways, my dear, but I have never been accused of slinking. Matthias was a natural slinker.'

'And this...this was before your time at Oxford?' I asked. 'When you were classmates with the Earl?'

Mr Gout gave a humourless smile, a phantom of the cheerful grins so usually attached to his chubby features. 'Why don't you ask the *real* question, Clementine, my dear?'

So I did. 'How old *are* you, Mr Gout?'

'In truth,' he said. 'I do not know. How old did the Earl's son say the Earl was?'

'Eighty-nine.'

'Then it would seem that I am about eighty-nine. Though I cannot say for sure. There is a period of my life, my dear, that I am afraid to say remains clouded to me.'

'Does this have to do with the curse, sir?' I asked.

He nodded. 'I believe so, yes. You see, one day, many years ago now, I awoke with no idea where I was, no idea how I had come to be there, and, perhaps most important of all, no idea *who* I was. Thankfully, some of my memories returned to me in time. But there remains a blank spot. Along, of course, with the other effects of which you are already aware.'

'That you cannot sleep under a proper roof,' I said. 'And…and that you cannot remember where your house is.'

Mr Gout nodded again. 'It might be more proper to say that I do not remember where my family's house is. For it is the same home in which I grew up that is lost to me.'

I thought about that for a minute. 'So that would be in the same village where your brother…' I found I could not finish the sentence. But Mr Gout knew what I meant.

'Yes. The very one. It is the strangest feeling. I remember growing up there, at least in abstract terms. I remember the terrible events that followed, in part, and a little of my life afterwards. I remember my first steps upon the road to this existence of magic and mystery that I now find myself in. But I cannot remember *where*, and believe me, I have tried, my dear. Oh, how I have tried! But I could never find any trace.'

'Couldn't you just ask someone?' I said. 'Someone who knew you back then, I mean. Like the Earl?'

'Well, up until now, it has been a moot point,' he said. 'For my memories of that time are clouded at best. I remember my family, none of whom still live. But more than that…is difficult. For instance, I knew I had attended university, or at least I felt I had. But I never could remember which one, or indeed in which year. Our friend the Earl's son has answered those questions, at long last. But as for anybody else who knew me from that time, I've never met one. '

'But now you have!' I said excitedly. 'The Earl knows all about what happened to your brother. He may know where your home is too!'

Mr Gout took a deep breath. 'So it would seem.'

'You don't…you don't seem very excited about it,' I said.

'In truth, Miss Trussel, I sometimes wonder if I am not better off as I am. I do not know what I have forgotten. I do not know if I will like what I find, should I recover what I've lost.'

'Surely it is better to know the truth of a thing,' I said.

This time, my master smiled a true smile. 'Spoken with the wisdom, and dare I say naivety, of youth, my dear. But of course you are right.'

'So…what does that mean?' I asked.

'It means, my dearest Clementine, that I need to go and see a man about a house.' And he winked at me.

THE END

Trussel and Gout will return in:
Castle Gout's Peculiar Petunias

Turn the page for a free book!

FREE BOOK

Sign up to the M.A.Knights VIP readers club at www.maknightswrites.co.uk and get a free prequel book!

MORE BOOKS BY M.A.KNIGHTS

*Trussel and Gout:
Paranormal Investigations*

The Pig In The Derby Hat

Something In The Woodshed

ACKNOWLEDGEMENT

As usual I could not have written this book without the unending support of my wife. How she puts up with my obsessive author brain I will never know.

Special thanks to Hanna and her input on the first draft of this story. Your encouragement is invaluable.

Thanks once again to my editor Nick, who made this story shine. As usual, any remaining mistake are mine alone.

Finally, thanks to you, the reader. Without you this would all be a waste of time. So thanks for coming on this adventure with me.

ABOUT THE AUTHOR

Hello. I'm M.A.Knights, an English writer living in the glorious countryside of wild west Wales. Here the rugged cliffs, rolling hills and ever-changing sea inspire the worlds of my creation. After achieving a BSc in Countryside Conservation and an MSc in Geographic Information and Climate Change, I realised I am, in fact, not a scientist at all. It's the what-do-you-call-it? ... memory! Not what it used to be, don't you know? And what with all those numbers and things ... dreadful! Simply dreadful. So I've left the data crunching to those cleverer than I and instead have returned to the fantastical imaginings of my youth. I hope one day to lose myself in a world of my own creation.

Head to www.maknightswrites.co.uk for more information.

Printed in Great Britain
by Amazon